David Mar studied English and American literature before becoming a journalist and a writer. He's a proud dad and a nature-lover. He has published poetry folios on various subjects ranging from isolation to grief, love, nature and politics. His fiction work flirts between real-life crimes, horror and the supernatural, where he celebrates the ordinary everyday lives that make the extraordinary possible. His recent work explores dystopia and gender identity.

In remembrance of the love that created my little sweetie.

David Mar

Hollow Man

Austin Macauley Publishers™
London • Cambridge • New York • Sharjah

A CIP catalogue record for this title is available from the British Library.

ISBN 9781528953863 (Paperback)
ISBN 9781528954037 (ePub e-book)

www.austinmacauley.com

First Published 2023
Austin Macauley Publishers Ltd®
1 Canada Square
Canary Wharf
London
E14 5AA

I would like to thank the publisher for their insightful vision and their laudable enterprising spirit, which testifies to their passion for books. I would like to thank the church of my little town for their insatiable passion, dishevelled faith and knowledge of the unseen, as well as Mary, her family and my friends for accompanying me with their kindred spirits.

Spider House

'Who ever asked a ghost for a witness statement?' I said, searching for atonement, as I stared at the Jehovah's Witness straight in the face…

'But is this your house?'

I felt my lips moving.

'Yes, this is my house, but I've just returned from a long trip…' I said mechanically.

'You know Jesus died for our sins, right?'

It seems I had nothing better to do than stand in front of my Edwardian town house in my pyjamas. As I sat on piles of burner logs, memories of my house seemed to writhe in the air from under the English moss. It was raining, and gusts of wind were whipping the landscape into dishevelled and shadowy shapes.

The house hadn't been inhabited for a while. If I once embraced blindly the neat varnish of positivism, and the organised dilapidation of the UK's lifestyle, it's because Koroshiya and I had elected this building as our home a long time ago…

Now that the playful dappling of a spell of sunshine pierced through rims of vegetation above my jellied head, I remembered the first time I walked in to visit the house… It seemed like a hazy waking dream at first, like a distant pitter-patter on the window of time… Jehovah's witnesses were sat at a table in the garden, waiting:

'What is this all about?' I asked. 'Who are you waiting for?'

I didn't expect them to be able to answer that question, as I, the owner, could barely muster an explanation for this incongruous situation… They just sat there nodding…

'I locked myself out! Who are you waiting for in my garden, anyway?' I asked. But it was obvious that I would not get an answer… I grumbled some insult and turned away from this ridiculous vision… My eyes rested on the drenched, weathered and cracked mustard door, under a period balustrade, at the top of the porch…

As this vision threatened to fade in the morning mists, I was told things had gone wrong, that I had lost the plot, that I would be able to understand in a few years, but that there was little chance the plot would unravel straight away… A trust had been set up by the conscientious but conservative curator of my museum of personal memories… I was to wait for him eating a spam burger according to voiceless instructions… The four Jehovah's witnesses were still nodding.

'What? Are you still there?' I shouted as I woke up, startled by the rain on my face.

I had come back to see 'Spider house' for one last time before selling it. Somehow, my key didn't work in the lock, so I had to call a locksmith.

'It's quite common. It could have been burglars trying to jump the lock,' he had said.

On that sunny August afternoon, I had dozed off on the pile of burner logs, waiting for him. I've always been able to sleep anywhere, in any position.

◆◆◆

'I am telepathic,' I said to Koroshiya on our first date.

We met in the local Evangelist church. One wintry weekend, we were strolling up and down a salt-gnawed Victorian pier in the North-West of England. She commented on the rectitude of the Victorian bridge's architectural lines while I marvelled at the overcast sky… The rain drizzled through our clothes and into our head… I speak of a love bubble where two beings fall ever closer to the precipice of a paradise, ready to spread their wings and melt into each other's eyes…

A handful of golden chips later, we were whisked into a side street hotel by night angels… We made love till the morning lights and woke up in a beautiful world come true, as lovers do. And over a copious English breakfast, Koroshiya asked me candidly:

'What does telepathy involve exactly?' she said in the Victorian peer café.

'It's about communication between brain waves…' I said authoritatively, trying to fight back a pork cartilage left in a sausage by a daydreaming factory worker…

'It's communication by other means than the senses, with someone that is far away or not so far away, but not with you, not right now…'

'You mean pathetic,' she said jocularly, clenching my arm, like old couples do… We strolled back to my aged and rusty VW, laughing, lost in translation…

I loved Koroshiya from the start… I loved her delicate traits, her dark hair and salty lips, her endearing eyes which always seemed to absolve my dissolute eccentricities… We moved into a house in the beautiful Peak District three months later.

The house was perfectly designed to protect our love.

It was a small two up, two down end of mews stone cottage. There was a reception/dining room, a lounge, a room for my office, a splendid bathroom, decorated with natural stone and tiles in a beautiful blue wave pattern, oak floors all over the ground floor rooms, and two carpeted stairways with carved wooden balustrades leading to the two distinct parts of the house, in fact two cottages knocked down into one.

There was a disused back garden, only accessible with a ladder over a limestone's wall, and a small patio where a bush of pink rambler Dorothy Perkins tea roses grew wildly. There was also a fountain with an electric motor that kept switching on without notice. The bijou kitchen had the bare essentials: a sink, a gas/electric oven, a space for a washing machine and handmade pine cupboards.

The very first weeks were idyllic… We cleaned the house from top to bottom. Koroshiya got so carried away that she cotton-budded the corners of the white wooden Georgian windows for a whole day. It was our first home… We loved every nook and cranny. It was a bridleway known only by horse riders and ramblers… We bought our own furniture: a brown leather sofa, a seductively bulbous Dunhelm green floor lamp, a German oak table, an oak queen-size bed, and an Ottoman chest and green cushions to match the lamp.

Looking back, we never even thought of a housewarming party. Our happiness was exclusive… We often talked ourselves to sleep, deep into the night, inebriated by grand ideas and theorems…

One Sunday morning, we were walking hand in hand, commenting on the strangely quiet, yet picturesque small-town canvas, as if we had been parachuted in a pre-Raphaelite heaven… Our first encounter with the locals was an old man who remarked leeringly:

'You smile too much.'

This remark would not have stayed on my mind if it hadn't been for the fact the old dandy wore an anachronic lampshade moustache and a blue silk ascot. Although Koroshiya brushed away this little incident with an offhand remark, deriding the lunatic as a one-off insane loner, I had been morbidly stung in my happiness for a reason I could not fully grasp…

My obdurate fixation on this incident lasted for several weeks, and was deeply unsettling… First impressions last, and I believed the town had sent us his chief killjoy officer to tell our love wasn't welcome.

We were soon swallowed up by the daily grind of our devouring careers… Koroshiya was an astrophysicist and taught at Manchester University. She had deep-rooted unflinching views about the world and its creation. Besides being a sensitive being, she was also a Shinto Buddhist.

I couldn't let go… What manner of weirdo would proffer such an ominous prophecy point-blank to a complete stranger? How can one smile too much?

Old houses are testament to the passing of time: still vessels of time made solid, but first houses acquire glimmering magical qualities as you pin up your filial ambitious for the future of your family on their walls. Windows become eyes and doors that smile on in its inhabitants with a protective wink.

We were supposed to live our fairy tale peacefully until our new home would one day protect a baby and a family.

One night, as I was getting ready to go to bed and clean my teeth in the bathroom, I heard Koroshiya scream… I ran down the stairs, through the living room and the lounge, and up the second flight of stairs to find she was coiled in fear, in the corner of the landing, outside the master bedroom…

'What happened?' I asked her.

Speechless and horrified, she pointed to the bed. It was covered with a thick blanket of black spiders! I could barely believe my own eyes. The sheer crawling multitude beggared belief. I took Koroshiya's hand and walked her out of the bedroom, comforting her with reassuring words. Since she wouldn't calm down, I took her to a hotel for the night.

On the way to the city centre, she explained how five minutes earlier, she had gone into the upstairs bedroom to fetch a cardigan. Everything was normal, except for the cold she felt in the bedroom. She checked the radiators. They were red hot. Koroshiya was sensitive to cold.

'I know Koro, I saw them too!'

Beyond the horrifying sight, she had been stung in her happiness too.

At the hotel, she described how my mood had changed since we moved in. She decided that there was something utterly spooky about the house that only materialised with the spider incident. I thought that we were being victims of a collective hallucination, but her rational mind could not accept my version. She described how I began pretexting an apophatic vein, a contagious melancholy that had rubbed off on me from the old industrial Peak District town. I blamed isolation. She even wondered if I had second thoughts about us moving together. She shared her concerns with me on the way to her friend's house, the following day:

'There's something about this house that we missed. You wanted to live here, now I feel guilty for yielding to your wish so easily. I should have been more circumspect.'

She grumbled, short of answers. I was a sucker for pointing a finger, she said.

'I'm sure my father will appreciate your blaming me for moving into this house, whereas he so kindly helped us with the deposit.'

'Those things are strange, but you can't make too much of it. It doesn't mean the house is haunted,' said her friend, a property surveyor, in a thick northern Irish accent. His cauliflower ears moved up and down as he spoke.

We didn't talk on the way back home… As I opened the door of spider house, with some anticipation, debating the ludicrous spider event with the haunting feeling that I could expect a wet blanket of crabs any minute, we found that everything had returned to normal. But as days went by and nothing untoward happened, it wasn't fear that I began to see clouding her green eyes, but annoyed despondency at the realisation we didn't feel alone anymore, that our home wasn't exclusive to us, that it was haunted.

After a breadth of strange physical and sensorial phenomena that irreversibly tainted our love for our new house, I understood the house did not want her… Koroshiya wasn't welcome. As a matter of fact, any female visiting would be persona non grata…

On a rainy Saturday, in autumn, two of Koroshiya's friends were invited to dinner…

Masako and Sayori were in their 20s: two Japanese girls from university with laughter in their eyes, eager to discover their friend's new home.

The dinner had started with the girls recollecting shared memories, laughing at the little serendipitous details of their existence in the UK. The pork loin Koroshiya had cooked for hours was a complete fiasco, however. As they sat at the table to a rare pork loin, Koroshiya fumbled for excuses…

Suddenly, we all felt so cold that each of us had to wear blankets over our shoulders while eating!

But Masako, one of the girls grew suddenly so hot that she started removing her clothes one by one. Before our incredulous eyes, she was soon naked, smiling ostensibly, while intermittently biting into her raw medallion of pork, which she held in her hands.

Koroshiya quickly covered her body with a blanket as she kept laughing and clinching voraciously at her piece of raw meat. The tableau of Masako naked eating a loin remained as a vivid memory, but not all of the strange happenings in our house were humorous…

Despite the idyllic sceneries and wonderful walks, we soon realised that the canvass of English culture made people crass and narcissistic. In our eyes, even the outside world became ominous and threatening. We blamed the lack of spirituality in everyday life in our little town on the inhabitants' insistence on self-interest and practical matters.

Our neighbours were either alcoholic, bipolar or aspiring middle class who were emulating established recipes for pessimism.

Two months passed without supernatural incidents. Suddenly, Koroshiya decided overnight that she was cool with extramarital affairs – she had somehow become a fatalist – so she would refrain from sexual activity and told me to seek pleasure in other females' company to the condition that I would need to be honest about it. We'd known each other for four years and I'd never been unfaithful. I thought our love was exceptional. I would have been enchanted with this extramarital freedom, had it not been for the fact that she didn't seem to care at all. How did that thought ever come to enter her mind? I wondered… How could she believe that I could be interested in anyone else or even suggest that I should see other girls?

Again, focused on my ego and my new sexual lease of life, I lost sight of the irreconcilable circumstances that had driven a wedge between us. My desperate reassurances on the fact we were better than this house fell upon a death ear.

One morning, I received a cheque from one of my customers. It was in April… I had been working as a trend consultant for a large pharmaceutical company. By then, Koroshiya had had to travel suddenly to visit her grandmother who was hospitalised in Japan…

I went out to buy some groceries… I remember carefully laying down the cheque that had come through the post, on the reception room table, by the dining room windowsill… When I came back, I took my bunch of keys out of my pocket but struggled to open the door as I realised that my Yale brass key was bent at 45°. Logically, only a force applied by mechanical means could have bent that yellow Yale key. Yet, it had been in my pocket all the time while I was shopping. It was a hot day, sure… But the key was good as new and of good stock. Besides, by English standard, it could not have been more than 80°F. I assumed naively at first that the key could have been directly exposed to the sun; that somehow, it had melted enough to bend in my pocket. Even Koroshiya, had she been around, could not have denied that it was physically and scientifically impossible…

As if that wasn't enough, I found the cheque on the floor, torn in two… I was bemused but resolved to find out the truth about those spirits that inhabited the house. I could have mistaken this envelope for unsolicited advertising and torn it apart myself without noticing, but a cheque? The letterhead and envelopes were unmistakably quaint, I remembered laying down the envelope carefully on the table… The other explanation was telekinetics, but, then, why would I want to do that to my own key and money?

Telekinetics is a different world altogether… It wasn't the best reason for this uncanny occurrence, but I was short of answers… I didn't believe I had such powers anyway… There was no readily available explanation…

After a series of similar incidents, I came to the conclusion that spirits were setting me challenges… The spider invasion was a plague. God wanted to set his people free… I began a long fast to understand why our house didn't want my Koroshiya. It had to be some sort of a foreboding…

I had begun resenting her weakness and her incidental reclusive moods as she convinced herself I didn't love her anymore. No matter how hard I tried to play it down, to reassure or comfort her, we were trapped in incomprehension… Before her last trip, her silent resignation and cold pragmatism became irreconcilable. We were strangers in our own house. Koroshiya lived in one part of the house and I, in the other… We barely talked to each other.

By then, we had become total strangers living in closed quarters. Deep inside, I knew that Koroshiya would never return.

Meanwhile, every time a spider would surface on a wall or a board, I would pick it up, and instead of crushing it like a scared housewife, I would trap it into a box and release it into the wild again, purposefully sending a message to the spider genus that I wasn't a threat. As ludicrous at it sounds, it worked…

At this stage, I had no other rationale at hand but to believe my own lucubration.

Jellied Head

I sometimes think our love must have been quite weak for evil to pulverise it into dust with such crass…
When I began to have enough time on my hands, my investigation later identified who, or rather what was behind this malevolent act of sabotage and destruction.

I did wonder if I wasn't unconsciously pushing Koroshiya away, but try as I might, I couldn't find any reason why I would have chased the love of my life away from me.

In June, I made an appointment with Mrs Jones, psychotherapist in Hayfield, a little village eight miles from my house. Hayfield was a tranquil and isolated village at the bottom of Kinder Scout, the highest peak in the region. Her practice was easy enough to find. The building entrance was unmistakably gaudy, as if it advertised a fashion clothing store, or an art gallery. But by July, it was obvious to us both that I wasn't suffering from any delusion or psychosis. I was however given advice to trust my feelings and engage with them.

I should have known what was going on and I was angry for not seeing it sooner… According to Mrs Jones, my unconscious could have been the reason for all these events.

Koroshiya and I divorced and settled. I re-mortgaged the house and went on with my life… Despite my sadness at our separation, I remained placid and determined to see my investigation through… In the twilight of my solace, despite Koroshiya's painful absence, I managed to gather my wits and make progress… This must have been the hardest time of my life. Indeed, in the dead of the following winter, free of the spiders, I had now a new manifestation to contend with…

Before long I believed that the floor of my extension, between the first-floor bathroom and my kitchen ceiling on the ground floor, was infected with rats… I could clearly hear them scuttle away over my head as I banged on pans and frying pans to dispel the annoying noises. I investigated my kitchen ceiling by tearing a few plasterboards down, but found no trace of the rodents. Just as I thought, I was the subject of auditory hallucinations so vivid that my immediate reaction was to believe in their physicality, every phenomenon slowly bringing me closer to insanity…

Now, I could be certain that a spirit was nagging me… One morning, I woke up to find a white tissue on the top of the kitchen bin, inside the sink cupboard… This time, it was visual… I had been dreading this moment. The spirits inhabiting my house had blown me a raspberry. It was embarrassing… How could a mouse or a rat do that for fun?

It occurred to me that I might have been sleepwalking. So that I dismissed the white tissue on the top of the bin event as one slip of the mind occurrence. But the noises from the kitchen went on during the day…

Rather than giving in to neurosis – country mice were an ordinary sign in the countryside and not necessarily a manifestation of a spirit – I resolutely called in the builders in the dead of January… Mid-way through the works, I asked them to let me know in case they found any signs of the rodents. There should have been traces of their passage: droppings, skeletons, feathers, and God knows what, but no signs. I realised by then that I had been the sole spectator of a spirit circus show. The noises eventually stopped. Although I managed to fight this plague away, I went from bibulous aesthete to stern ascetic again, but this time, out of choice… I was determined to see my investigation through.

This also coincided with my baptism as a disciple of Christ in the local Baptist church, which by all standards, could be rightfully perceived as a last-ditch effort to find some spiritual meaning out of madness.

I could have sold the house. I could have moved on, but I was convinced that I shouldn't leave or couldn't convince myself that I could leave. I was trapped.

Once the house was exorcised by the local pastor, I began missing the spirits that had inhabited it. After all, as preposterous as it may sound, those spirits had kept me company… That is when I felt the need to investigate my gifts. The theory of it all, the science behind them needed to be laid down. Since I couldn't get rid of them, I had to learn how to live with them.

After all, resolving an occurrence didn't mean that the haunting was over.

I began to see that even human beings communicate with each other through spiritual and even supernatural means. It is not only a prerogative of mothers to feel something has happened to their child at an incredible distance, in some time continuum that they share intimately…

Turtles… Hatchlings emerge from their eggs and thanks to the high iron content in their brain – some call it hematite – they are able to imprint their location and follow the itinerary their parents followed themselves. They learn how to navigate magnetic fields to return to their own breeding grounds thanks to the same iron in their brain…

In humans, this gift is somehow subdued and undeveloped, males in particular, whereas women are commonly attributed a sixth sense. Déja vu, precognition, premonitions all fall under the same category: the unexplained.

Yet, the psychotherapist explained to me how the collective unconscious described by Carl Jung could shed a dim light on those phenomena, as a mystical world inhabited by archetypes and ancestral knowledge was already there, even before our birth.

The soul taps on those resources without our knowing…

I felt like a placid and sickly Darwin; a visionary on the verge of a breakthrough which I could not make sense of yet…

I began to form the theory that humans also follow magnetic fields if they choose to… Cats or animals find their way home no matter how far they are dropped. Those extraordinary phenomena characterise all species alike, even the least sensitive and the less intelligent ones. For humans, we talk of a God leading his people; for animals, it's instinct… For my part, I believe that we are both instinctive humans and religious animals.

I would once be the catalyst of an animal's spirit… It was one of my most interesting and confusing cases during what I call my 'clinical training'… The spirit of a dog took hold of me… It made me bark every morning… Of course, I don't mean I literally barked like a dog. Rather, I yelled hollow and angry words, vociferating insults at my bare walls. I now know that in the morning, I would bark because I was hungry or for no apparent reason other than a cat's paw print or the smell of a feral cat's piss within a few meters of my front door, I would open my jaws and uncontrollably shout insanities. At times, for no other reasons than hearing birds eking out borrowed times in my gutters, indulging in innocent cackling and prattling on the flashing of my roof, I would fly off the handle unexpectedly…

That is when I discovered that spirits use our instincts to communicate…

There's an open door we crave to leave ajar when we are vulnerable and ready to believe in anything. I had become a recipient of a dog's spirit entangled with its owner's, but it took me months to sort out the wheat from the chaff.

Since my ex-wife's departure, I had become obsessed with the spirits of an old woman and her dog only to find out that they had been living in my stone cottage in 1875. I couldn't find a great deal of information on her, except that she was a teetotal protestant pioneer who traded as a confectioner. I could not dismiss the dogged hallucinations without finding evidence for it. After all, a single woman must have needed some sort of comfort and safety during those dark rural nights. I gnawed on that bone for a few weeks…

I finally found out her identity looking at the deed of my neighbour's house where the main plot used to be. It was now split in two different parcels, but the library census records helped refine my search down to this charitable protestant who had owned the plot in the 19th century… The departed

Victorian activist even specifically stipulated in her deed the caveat that no alcohol should be made on the premises…

No wonder I always sat in between old-timers at church, I thought the following week, while attending a young pastor's service who was announcing the rebranding of the old local Wesleyan Sabbath School after 140 years…

How exactly did I come to know that church, I wondered? Was it another invitation from the world of spirits? An enthusiastic evangelist used to wave at me while I was smoking on my doorstep (I used to smoke at the time but stopped when Koroshiya left). Sherley, a 60-year-old hippy turned eccentric Baptist had meek manners and a flimsy voice. She kept inviting me to church… It sure felt good sharing my Sunday morning depression with others, so much so that I became a regular… Her group bon vivant of a husband, Mark, also went by the name of "bubble man", as he ran a children entertainment act where he used a wind-propelled machine among other contraptions, optical illusions and eco-friendly devices.

We not only talked about re-branding that week, but also charity… I decided I had vested interests in this church since I used to go there when I was alive…

It all made sense… I was now in between two waters as a psychic on a learning curve into the arcane world of life and death…

The church also owned an eponymous cafe that served cinnamon toasted teacakes, sundaes and cappuccino coffee, sprinkled with chocolaty jazz litanies and syrupy choruses served on a shameless bed of malingering gossip…

One morning, I walked into the café in a rage… Instead of making my kitchen watertight (my leaking bathtub stood just above my small bijou kitchen), John, the churchwarden and builder, had created a Van Gogh scene… My cabinets were at different angles, doors hardly shut properly, and the sink taps faced the user at weird angles. It happened that the simpleton responsible for that DIY fiasco lived just above the cafe, in a small one-bedroom flat he rented all expenses paid by the church. Despite the botched job, the positive argument against murder was that the rat problem was solved since I had confirmation that no rodents ever lived in my kitchen ceiling…

It wasn't the first time I had to use extra-help to finish off a spirit channelling. I would later use builders to revamp haunted houses and dislodged any residual spirit… Spirits attach to objects and furniture or furnishings their owner have touched during their life. It is an alchemy that follows a secret geometry. This is how the old lady's spirit must have manifested itself, I thought, once I had calmed down in front of a piping hot cappuccino… She must have been aggravated by the displacement of stones in what used to be her garden or even the presence of another soul on her old territory. If a churchgoer's spirit could do that, I dreaded what criminals' spirit could do… Yet, statistically, the odds are not always straightforwardly in favour of the righteous dead. Criminal minds surround their lives and thoughts with multiple decoys and personalities, and this is reflected in the fabric of their after-world spiritual persona. The one they call Satan comes to mind…

I always thought that communication with the afterlife was a sham and that spirit manifestations were a normal consequence of the living's insanity or boredom… That is until I had no choice but to exorcise such a spirit in my own house.

I rest my new line of trade as a psychic medium on the premise that untimely deaths more often leave the relatives, friends or known persons clutching at straws, craving for an answer. One criminal, in particular, turned out to be a real conundrum… I had just started working on a case of possession. Some men leave unachieved works, whether good or bad. It wasn't for me, now a psychic by trade, to discriminate… After all, my service only involved offering peace of mind. The justice system usually provides this in a selective and reasoned manner, yet what if it fails? What if, in the case of a sudden untimely death – which is the alma mater of all psychic detectives – motive is never found? What about unexplained suicides, unsolved murders, disappearance cases gone cold?

One morning, I was sat in the church cafe, the one linked to the evangelist church. I opened the posh paper, past the usual royal curtsies, romantic psychodramas, and cracks at the lefties; there it was: between the cruise advertisements and the jingoistic Spartan sports pages… A Nietzschean recluse chased by the police for several murders… I remember distinctly the headlines amidst the background gossip about the church rebranding…

A frozen body, discovered on the mountain called Kinder Scout, in 2012, were still puzzling the press who were trying to revive the story.

I had been chosen to solve a mystery by an invisible hand.

◆◆◆

That macabre revival was due to the fact that another frozen body was found under snow in the winter of 2016… This time, it was identifiable. It belonged to a Victorian lady whose identity remained under seal.

Kinder Scout, the nearby mountain, is not high enough to be crowned with perpetual snow, but the winter of 2012 had been exceptionally cold. In 2016, less so. How the body became frozen puzzled one journalist from the Metro paper, in particular.

Meanwhile, a recluse who liked to fancy dress as a werewolf frightened the hell out of ramblers on Kinder Scout. This could have remained a jocular hoax if two women, down in the village, at the foot of the High Peak Mountain, in the North-West of England, had not disappeared from their homes…

The body discovered in 2012 belonged to an unidentified Victorian lady. It had been preserved. There was no explanation for its preservation. None at all.

Both journos and police were baffled.

The case was therefore the ideal wild card to make a name for myself as a psychic.

I decided to ramble over the peat and wind-slashed heather-strewn moorland trails one summer morning… Clouds of spinning droplets swirled with the wind over the muddy trails, a few miles away from the fear-stricken village of Hayfield where wind-torn clouds clung on to the summit of desolated knolls.

As the minerals-charged rain dripped with harrying relentlessness into my walking gear, I began to resent my knee-jerk decision to scour the gloomy plateaus of carboniferous Kinder Scout. I suddenly correlated what I had read in the press that morning and the flash vision of a woman dressed in Victorian clothes walking in the main street, flanked by a tall guy in a three-piece suit, petticoat and a top hat, that I had seen the same day, while desperately trying to enjoy a day-off by reading the press at the Church café. I had originally thought they were a couple going to a fancy-dress party but no one else inside the café had seen them.

I now realised under the drenching rain that a mid-week afternoon fancy dress party was not just an unlikely occurrence but another trick played by the after-world. This was the first psychic clue in my criminal investigation, however. It meant the Victorian lady must have known her killer, if indeed, murder there was…

At this stage, the cause of death was uncertain; yet, the article was adamant there had been foul play. On top of the incredible condition of the corpse, the DNA analysis revealed that she had been last alive in 1888, August 30 or 31, date of her disappearance.

Whatever I had read was obviously playing on my mind… And after a few days, I decided to lead a factual investigation… I would follow the fallout of this discovery in the village's meeting places, cafés, restaurants, pubs, and even the Conservative club, partly to try and extract some precious gossip from the local busybodies. But more often than not, I would come home with an empty bag, as a cloak of silence remained irremediably wrapped around the mysterious disappearances…

I has to allow the tenuous link between the present and the past to be woven by the same invisible hand that had gifted me this case in the first place…

With the July rains, the subdued atmosphere that had followed the press hype thinned out into a daily routine of oblivion. It wasn't until dinner, after another arduous walk, that I found some water to my mill, several weeks later… I had just sat down in front of a pint, waiting for my meal, in the local watering hole down the twitchel-strewn lane, behind the old mill's Torr bridge, when my foreign accent raised suspicions… A few inquisitive dogged natives darted their scient looks through the thick brooding atmosphere of the local pub. Before I knew it, a dribbling drunk wearing a fiddler cap sat in front of me.

'Supwiyou, Gromit?'

'What do you mean?' I asked slightly taken aback at the familiarity.

'Just messing with you, do you mind?' He put his cap on the wooden table, intent on settling in.

'You're that psychic fella, aren't you? Yeah, that's right, I remember you asking questions around,' he said, sizing me up.

'I'll be damned,' I said theatrically. 'How can you possibly know that? You're the one who's psychic, mate!'

'That lady they found was one of my ancestors… As a matter of fact, I know you're full of shit… So what brings you here?'

'I'm not sure… It's been hectic recently as you know… I haven't been out of my cave for a while, I guess I needed to see faces, and good-hearted people like yourself,' I said sardonically. 'So you know the victim?'

'I'm good-hearted all right, you bastard!'

He snatched his cap and left, cheering his drinking buddies on his way out.

What an idiot, I thought… I wasn't sure what he meant to tell me, but his sudden departure raised a few eyebrows at the bar, namely one stocky fellow with a shaven head who turned around to speak to me:

'Don't mind him… It's the beer talking, he's not a bad egg; he just had his fill of foreigners, that's all.'

'Really?' I said grittily.

It remained the tipple was excellent… I ordered another pint and started chatting with the stocky pundit, a gardener whose obvious love for nature drew him incessantly back to the waitress's voluptuous curves… I soon forgot why I was there after two pints and made a beeline to the loo due to a hereditary small bladder. As I stepped out of the men's, another fellow engaged me on the picturesque merits of his native Hayfield. I listened to his slurring blog-in-the-bog PR until I remembered my agenda: the disappearances…

'No one knows; I wouldn't take it seriously… Two females have disappeared. Probably connected… Some lesbians doing a runner… You never know, these days…'

They all chuckled in unison as we emerged from the men's.

'But now you mention it', said the gardener, 'my dad told me about a similar case he heard of when he was a boy, up there in the sticks, about females disappearing, I mean. They never caught the guy; they were even told by the cops there was a werewolf roaming at night… Especially on windy nights over Jacob's ladder and beyond… What a load of rubbish!'

'Local folklore,' said another…

'Police brutality, I'd say,' said a younger man, ordering an umpteenth pint.

‘Mind you,’ said another, ‘there’s no smoke without fire… Last year, sheep were slaughtered near Barber booth…’

I listened to their conversation for a while until the sheep’s massacre turned into a justification for the war in the Middle East…

On my way back home, a lukewarm mizzle brought me back to my senses… A group of youngsters were walking in silence, barefooted, over the slippery-slabbed Torr River bridge. By then, I had some inkling that my first psychic crime investigation would be one of my most trying and interesting cases…

◆◆◆

Koroshiya and I had lived in Spider house together for four years… By the time of her departure, the house had been cleared of its past. But the town around our house still lived in the industrial era and those forlorn lives spent at the grinding textile and paper mills had echoes in every wall. Like an onion, the parochialism of the town seemed to ooze under multiple layers of hypocritical protocols about the grandeur of its past.

‘Nothing new under the sun’, I used to say to Koroshiya who resented the locals’ lack of mundanity. ‘It’s quite normal for a semi-rural town to be parochial, you will grow into it,’ I kept repeating…

On the other hand, my uncanny foreignness was a unique observatory position to observe the world around me. I could choose to take part, indulge in local banter or not, relate to local history or not, in short, make use of the chameleon’s privilege to blend in or not. Why didn’t she? As a matter of fact, my life as a psychic in New Mills could not have thrived better with the harsh industrial past of its 15,000 inhabitants. The old Torr mill was a testament to the cruel era when children as young as eight were forced to work 12 hours a day… Some even died within the walls of those textile mills… Who remembers the little boy whose head was crushed under the spinning mule's wheels while he was cleaning it?

Walking across the old mill town and the remnants of its industrial past, I would sometimes be snatched into the time continuum of the spirit world.

My theory is that there are people chosen by God to channel those spirits back to the light. Being one of them would never make my life easy, I knew that… It threatened the ones I loved, and more often than not, forced me to ensure their protection far away from me. I believe it was the case with Koroshiya and the secret child she was bearing, Poppy….

Dwelling in the throes of countless moments of doubts beside myself, constantly hearing voices, being stirred by the fatality of strange lives, steered by spirits away from the here and now became my daily bread. I would find myself in another person's world as far from mine as an elected politician from his convictions, stuck in clapping moments of thunder between my own existence and others', eternally pussyfooting in the ethereal world…

Private Jones

Walloping thunderous clouds
Amidst the glaring night,
Bear silent shrouds,
And a painful craving for light…

What grows inside the cave of
human darkness?
Were we to discern matter in a
soul's crevice,
Our spirit would let in the scent
of life. In like a bayonet…

◆◆◆

He almost censored the early years of his life when he was a fugitive… He talked in swathes of luminous truth and yearning…

I listened to his crazy ramblings by the small fire he had lit on the heights of Kinder Scout, at the top of Jacob's ladder… That is where I followed his voice muttering with wuthering chaos, I, sleepwalking on the brink of sanity. I had mistaken him for the murderer of those women. I wanted to know everything. He told me he was expecting me… I broke the silence during a pause… The memories of his childhood were confused, I could see that… He was tormented because he could not remember the exact sequence of his wife's death… Was it before or after the war? He was staring at the stars around us when I asked him thoughtlessly:

'So you're a bit of a poet then?'

It was always going to be a monologue on my part, as his agenda didn't allow him to converse with the living… He knew me though even if he didn't know who I was… I looked at my walking boots, a lace had snapped. My head was still numb with the blow I had received… I owed my luck being alive to the newspaper clip of the identified body found on Kinder Scout which had slipped from my pocket during my fall. It was she. I had felt his fingers pulling the picture from my trousers' pocket as my senses were whittling away.

When I woke up, he was staring at the precipice, his arms wrapped around his knees… He had told me to shut up as he lit a fire. He had a gun. Yet, it was the weight of his soul that was overbearing, like shackles.

I stayed quiet and gathered some branches, picked up a few stones and fed the damned fire as he asked me to do… Gradually, long pregnant pauses cleared the air of mutual suspicion. I alluded to the Kinder Scout cases by means of small anodyne questions…

'Yep! You never know what happens behind closed doors…' he groaned. I poked the fire mechanically…he went on.

'Death is everywhere… As soon as you sit on a bench, in the countryside, after an assault, you realise this insect world is ready to feast on your body… It doesn't take long before they make their way under your skin to claim their territory…'

There was another short pause… He lit a cigarette…

'Ever since I was in the army, I was told to never engage your enemy unless you have surveyed the battlefield first.'

'You were in the army?' I heard myself ask. But he wasn't taking any notice of my questions…

'What happened in the Somme was unacceptable when you look into it. It's down to the brass… It's their fault. Human lives just didn't matter!'

I looked at the dreamy trees below, in the valley… He carried on the subject of his campaigns in France, in 1916. I was dumbfounded. I was talking to one of the pals!

'I was born in 1890…' he said, turning towards me. As intriguing as his accounts were to a modern man like me, it didn't take me long to cross read the situation. The 2018 press article did mention women's bodies being clothed in Victorian clothes, and this man sitting across the fire was from the early 20th century, so he must have been the son rather than the husband. My fingers were fidgety, as I twiddled my makeshift poke while he remained still as a dead stump. He had fought in the Somme, survived with just a shot to his leg and courtesy of repetitive bouts of trenches fever, had been hospitalised most of his service. He seemed animated with revenge…

The moustache, the long chisel-carved face and pale fingers of the WWI soldier slouched and arched over a dormant and sombre landscape smelling of peat, corpses and minerals. It all felt real…

Assuming he was twenty-five or thirty at the time of his death, he could not have committed the murders of the

Victorian era, as he was too young. I had not had any time to read the police reports nor the press articles about the recent discovery before heading for Kinder Scout that morning, as he had snatched the newspaper clip from my pocket… I could see it meant something to him…

If I was speaking to a spirit, I was safe because I could always escape from this timeless deadlock by waking up somehow, or at least that's what my subconscious was telling me… If I wasn't, I had to get out of there as quickly as I could as I was dealing with a lunatic… Would I ever wake up? Was I on safe grounds or even asleep? I was not afraid but… Could this Tommy be insane? Somehow, against all odds, I wanted him to be real…

'Get cover! You stupid sheep-shagger!' he shouted. I was woken up with a kick in the ribs. I had allowed myself to doze off… My head was already drowsy from the cold wind. I opened my eyes on his rotten teeth.

'Diane sauce? What? In the middle of this shithole, sorry, I forgot my virgin white serviette, sir!'

I sprang to my feet and walked out of this contrived nightmare… It was dawn. I got out of my camp bed, reflecting strangely that Taylorism had no place in fine cuisine… The next thing I knew, I was lying on a rock and could barely move my shoulder. All I saw was a Kestrel flying over me, as if it had been shaped out of the morning mist. Within seconds, nature awoke in so many sharp chirping and pure wild sounds that I had to recognise he had disappeared from sight. I breathed with a sense of relief, conscious of my sordid camper's accoutrement… But the voice echoed again, louder than ever:

‘Macadamia nuts? College certificates? Arm that machine-gun! You stupid plank!’

I rolled on my stomach, praying for his rotten face to leave me alone, find his grave and disintegrate.

‘It’s over!’ I yelled, panting; my heart beating out of my chest.

‘The war is over, please!’

I didn’t realise I had thrown my arms vehemently around while protesting… A bottle of wine rolled down a dry rivulet and went crashing in scintillating smithereens down into Jacob’s ladder’s darkness… I had been sleeping inches away from a sheer drop, above a rocky gash…

‘Accusing me of being a coward, strumpet, are you? Fancy walking erect in the line of fire watching your mates die by your side, do you?’

It was all over in an instant, I had to convince myself these voices were his last eructation in the night of time. The voice of Private Jones died away with the last echo of a crashing wine bottle… I walked away in the direction of the morning sun without looking back less I turned into those Kinder Scout stones… I walked miles and miles to get away from my cold nightmare down to Hayfield, then to New Mills without stopping, then through Thornsett and past the small graveyard… Eventually, I got home where I found my little garden in bloom… The luscious witch-hazel which promised bright yellow flowers during winter, the climbing rose bush, the fast-growing Leylandii conifers: at last, I found a respite in the garden of my thoughts…

◆◆◆

Coming down from a paranormal investigation is like cooking a steak… The meat needs resting at least for as long as it has been cooking. I now found myself aggravated with a potent headache. It didn't take me long to find out why, as I stroke the back of my skull to feel a new conspicuous bump… Yet, the sun was high. It was warm and the afternoon sun blessed my little patch with heavenly light… I uncorked a bottle of Merlot and laid down the details of my overnight encounter on Kinder Scout. After a few glasses, I felt the need to talk… Olivia, from Jamaica, had recently moved in at the old bank, a grade II listed building, according to a fun-employed Evangelist who deplored the Nubian's lack of interest for religion. According to her, her own daughter had had the same boyfriend for a week… 'Great news', I said mildly happy… She was hopeful they would get engaged soon. I was introduced… One early morning, the week before, I had seen yet another man coming out of her house… He looked twenty years older that her current boyfriend… Yeah, we all know what that means… Never mind, it remains the old slapper knew where Olivia lived…

Down High Street, a sketch-artist was drawing a row of terraced stone houses…

'Before they're demolished,' he said.

I had caught a glimpse of Olivia during the carnival… Her feline gait had attracted my attention as she was ambling down the thronged street holding a glass of white wine with a serene smile on her face, seemingly enjoying the pageant. Her voluptuous curves kept me awake the very same night. I laid down these very observations on a note to let her know… I distractedly slipped the note through her letterbox, but forgot to include my phone number… This oversight could only mean it was high time for a rest. But I was still buzzing, so I went back to my garden and my notebook and finished reporting on the previous night's experience…

What were the implications of this encounter for my own investigation into the Kinder Scout murders? I struggled to find any at first… Apart from a few bruises and a throbbing headache to remind me that if my experience had been all so tactile, I could only remember scraps of conversation and a few lurid fireside images… I wasn't really thinking; I was tired… What's more, I had qualms about making any connection whatsoever with a modern crime involving a WWI veteran… I pondered the possible connections watching a horse trotting away from a fresh road-apple… I couldn't think straight. Was I still thinking like a cantankerous old spinster?

After a fruitful and rejuvenating nap, I came up with the concept of hollowness.

'I am hollow,' I muttered in my couch, underneath a grey sheep's blanket, my head resting on two green pillows.

Babes are born without knowledge… If humans could suppress their learned identity, it would be possible for them to achieve hollowness, emptiness beyond identity, in order to accept the truth… Spirits inhabit this hollowness.

'Call me his hollowness!'

I said to the ingratiating green-eyed cat ogling at my interior behind my French door.

◆◆◆

"Frozen Georgian body discovery stuns bobbies."

The Victorian gutter press was flaunting its disassociated contempt over the whole affair without giving much evidence to chew on… On the other hand, it was adamant that the killer had to be at least six-foot-tall and a hermit.

As to modern press releases, they did mention the link with the Victorian era, in particular, one regional issue of a Manchester daily whose quality of reporting could always be relied upon.

According to the Metro, it seemed that the police had made the link because the MO was too similar to go unnoticed… Just like I did, the modern-day journalist must have dug the case up while googledigooking his way through the web after an over-indulgent takeaway dinner. He must have salivated on the paperclips from the Victorian era as I, a few days later…

Yet, no one came with a plausible explanation as to why the bodies had been preserved despite there being no perpetual snow or ice on Kinder Scout… The only scientific explanation was the use of an expensive form of cryogenetics, which, apart from being unavailable in the 19th century, was far-fetched.

The chief superintendent speaking on TV was very cautious, and did not mention the historical similarity on air, for fear of attracting jeers and sneers from the media, one must suppose.

'We are pursuing all possible leads in this case, including past cases that remain unsolved…'

But there it was: "including past cases that remain unsolved".

Say no more…

I learned through a personal contact of mine at New Mills constabulary, a short plumpy and indiscreet CSO who happened to be the boyfriend of a local artist of my acquaintance, that the police were looking at the old serial killer copycat possibility. In all evidence, the possibility of a time-traveller-cum serial killer had been dismissed. This was usually when my talents were needed…

My own research had brought me closer to Jones' past and the investigation had now fallen within my purview…

My census search revealed that the Hayfield Joneses were a family of bootleggers, one of whom was accused of murder, but the same man seemed to have died during WWI. The family estate now belonged to The National Trust…

It had been two days since my otherworldly interview with Jones. While I was recuperating, the official investigation on the last body hit a wall. The DNA matched no one, but the Victorian clothes were authentic. When I returned to Hayfield later that day, after quickly browsing through the press, rumours had been spreading around the village…

I had taken the Sett Valley trail on a sweltering day. It was unusual for the month of July and totally damning as far as climate change was concerned… I stopped for breakfast in the doomed village where the case was on everyone's lips since the recent drumbeating around the frozen body… Despite the harrying articles which blamed the police for their befuddled approach and the locals for not sharing what they knew, no one seemed to be disturbed by the fact the first body was that of a Victorian woman.

Everyone had dismissed the first case as a historical conundrum.

I sat down in Millie's café, all ears to the rumours… But it seemed as if all leisurely talk was banished in the reputable chocolatier… People kept their heads down, reading the press…

My search revealed an article which told how Jones's grave had been desecrated in the 1950s to the point a special military section had to be dedicated to him in the communal graveyard on account of his Victoria cross…

According to a 1954 article in the high peak advertiser incorporating the Chapel-en-le-Frith, Whaley bridge, New Mills and Hayfield advertiser, the village hoped this grave gesture would reconcile the Joneses with their past…

One distinctively ingenious editorial even correlated Jones' alleged killing frenzy with a series of disappearances that plagued the little mountain village in the 1950s and which displayed the same MO as the Victorian murder. It seemed people were thinking out of the box in the 1950's. Conversely, the arrogant modern media had little time for the supernatural.

Warm black pudding slices aside, the atmosphere was thick with suspicion and boiling with anticipation… If the article in question referenced the same MO several years later after Jones' death, in the same meek and gentle neighbourhood, it is to underline the fact that the 1950's disappearances remained unsolved. 50 years down the line, Jones' case was still vivid in some of the oldest locals' memory who had to admit that he could never have been the culprit, and had rightfully been reinstated as a bona fide war hero…

Millie's served fry-ups in an orderly small-town unostentatious manner. Walking towards St George's pub, where I would have more chance of finding out more, I stopped at the monument dedicated to the unknown soldier, and felt relieved my WWI buddy was not a criminal…

At the pub, where I often ended up after a long walk, I ordered the guest ale from the local brewery and started chatting to a middle-aged man who told me his experiences as an engineer in Europe. It's hard to explain after three pints to a near complete stranger why one needs to discard the senses and the intellect in order to exalt divine darkness and be whole with the primeval spirit. Indeed, I could always try and explain why I was here, at the foot of Kinder Scout, no one would ever believe me… Enthusiastic as my interlocutor seemed to be, I doubt his exhilarated nods meant he was in agreement with my hollow theories… He probably thought it was the beer talking…

Our conversation did not go unnoticed however, and one dapper old woman sifting soup through her newly acquired denture was not amused, so that jovial puns and colourful jokes around the world of spirits were soon replaced with more earthly conjectures…

'I know what's going on,' said one ruby red face by the dispenser machine…

'It's because some bloody immigrants have been put up at the old hall. I say leave the EU before it's too late!'

'Spot on!' said an older fellow, running thoughtfully his fingers around the rim of his pint glass.

'I wouldn't have said it better!'

But soon, the chatter subsided and the voice of a man whom everyone knew as the "councillor" resonated with gravitas:

‘I was told from the horse’s mouth that the investigation is going nowhere… Or rather, it seems to point to a 100-year-old case.’

‘Precisely!’ I said, joining in the local rant… Once I had explained where I came from and why, narrowly evading the usual quizzical questions incumbent on foreigners, I attempted to squeeze more local knowledge out of the wolf pack.

‘Well, if you want spirits, you’ve come to the right place. But I can’t make him out,’ said the owner as if he had analysed his own joke and, in retrospect, didn’t find it amusing.

‘Who’s that?’ said the councillor.

‘Well, the murderer of course!’

‘They won’t catch him,’ he said with his customary gruff…

‘He’s got to be foreign!’ said the ruby red face near the nuts’ machine…

‘Nevertheless, that leaves a few murders unexplained,’ said the councillor, now probing the bottom of his glass.

‘I reckon he’s local,’ said a young man wearing a tank top. He had obviously been working all day out in the sun.

‘Ok, enough of that!’ said the landlord, as he noticed a party who had just walked in his pub… The tipple council agreed unanimously that this was a sore subject that was best left open for further discussion *in camera.*

‘It remains,’ said the ruby red face near the nuts’ machine.

‘Jones’ granddaughter must be going through a rough time,’ pointing with his chin to the old lady looking down the bottom of her plate.

I was the only one to hear that, as everyone else had moved on to the world cup…

‘I beg your pardon,’ I said, ‘Do you mean Jones’ granddaughter?’

‘Yes, the one who lives above Millie’s…’

Mrs Jones

The staff was not surprised to see me again. In fact, the timid glassy blue-eyed waitress smiled melancholically…

'What is it regarding?'

'Well, I would like to say hello to Mrs Jones whom I haven't seen for years. Would it be possible to leave her a note?' I said to the girl, now absentmindedly drying mugs by the coffee machine.

'I am afraid she's gone away for the weekend to see some family.'

'Is she a guest here?' I asked

'Yes, she lives here permanently. Who's asking?'

I left my number on a note to Mrs Jones asking her if she could spare a few minutes to talk about the olden days…

To eat or not to eat, that is the question… Call me what you will, but Mrs Jones craved nothing less than justice for the wrongful accusations that her father suffered most of his veteran's life, and I, psychic by trade, could not deny her that. It was just a matter of convincing her that I was the right man for the job…

A few days later, I received a note through my letterbox… I was to meet Mrs Jones for breakfast at Millie's… The neat blue-inked handwritten invitation card came without an envelope.

◆◆◆

As I walked into the chocolatier, I imagined a little girl in a white crinoline cardigan, pausing for the annual school portrait, unaware of the sum of years that she would come to incarnate… This vision came as I spotted Mrs Jones in the far corner of the café… Although I didn't know her, I recognised the old lady eating soup at the St George's pub.

I knew I had to tell her something shocking enough to be let into her world without beating about the bush…

'Mrs Jones,' I said to the dignified matriarch sitting over a smoky cup of tea on a corner table, below a watercolour landscape painting of Crowden Brook and the Noe River…

'Your dad loves you. He wants you to know that.'

She squirmed at first. Her beady glassy eyes stared coldly at me for seconds that felt like Genesis… I sat on the next table… She lifted her cup of tea with her jaded wrinkled fingers. Then, she cleared her throat and slowly turned her whole body towards me…

'I know,' she said with a constricted smile.

It goes without saying we both knew any conversation of that kind could not take place in a café during a busy breakfast hour… I hesitated before opening my mouth again, but just as she was about to leave, she slid what seemed to be another business card on my table… This time, it had an address…

As I finished my breakfast, I looked closer at the card: Mrs Jones had been a member of the thrifty and bull-by-the-horns-grabbing Women's Institute…

What a symbolic era, I thought, devouring my breakfast… Women coming together with inventive manners to get the most out of rations, doing their bit for their country, emulating their queen… Epoch-making feminism…

I called the number as soon as my last bean vanished from the surface of my plate. Mrs Jones wasn't surprised; in fact, I was welcome to call on her that very afternoon…

I was ravished really… For my first criminal psychic investigation, it was rather going smoothly… I barely had to walk a few hundred yards to call on her, past the old post office and the butcher's… Eventually, I faced an impressive gate leading up to a mansion hidden behind a tree plantation that must have dated back to the Victorian era judging by the variety of trees: oaks, redwoods, pines and cypresses…

Mrs Jones' apartments were directly above the café, around a picturesque building serving as the surgery.

After a short pensive walk, I reached her front garden which was neatly trimmed… Pots and planters were filled with cyclamen and pansies while a climbing rose bush and a water-feature against the front wall created an idyllic scene of calm and tranquillity…

Mrs Jones opened the door. She wore the very same cardigan I'd seen in my perceptive vision of her as a little girl, before our encounter, at Millie's… I was shown into her reception room and waited patiently for a scintilla of curiosity, but she said nothing and vanished into her secret kitchen. She soon brought back some earl grey tea in a crockery set…

It was a dark and gloomy day, between frizzling heat and stormy clouds… She decided we should instead sit at the garden table despite the menacing storm. I had every intention of listening to her no matter how long it would take, but she cut to the chase after the usual ice-breaking small talk and pedigree fact checking…

'That's it? Surely, your assurance this morning… I knew where you were coming from…'

'I do appreciate, Mrs Jones… But it's quite a story really… Do you believe in ghosts?'

Of course, I had plenty in store for her… I could have started by explaining how my earthly mission as a spiritual antiquarian had led me here, but I had to devise a larger scheme to make compensation sound more like a natural end… In other words, I had to convince her that I needed more than a cup of tea and a piece of toast…

'Are you going to tell me what he said or not?'

I obliged at length… I was too eager to share my encounter with her father… I even recalled Jones' diatribe against the peddlers of modern religions: 'When you invoke the name of Jesus to carry out your evil deeds around the world, you might as well make Barabbas your saviour.'

'He said that?'

Jones' daughter bemused expression egged me on… She didn't know her father had a religious side… I also learned Mrs Jones was born in the 1920's and had been cast out of the Women's Institute in the late 50's, on account of her father being accused of murder. She had regained part of her estate under a scheme set up with a circle of lawyering friends and her children in the Manchester mills where, destitute, and disgraced, she had to work as a seamstress. A few hours passed in the stormy garden… We told each other everything…

'When I think about that moronic Victoria Cross forfeiture malarkey, it really makes me mad!' she said.

‘It was a sad affair.’ I said empathetically.

Jones’ Victoria Cross had been forfeited then reinstated. But I realised sitting through the tear-jerking annals of her dad’s life that her aim was not to clear her family name…

‘Do you know anything about those murders and those frozen bodies discovered on Kinder Scout last winter? I mean, how is it possible anyway, there isn’t any everlasting snow in Kinder Scout, is there?’

Mrs Jones pondered my rationalism and my European accent for a few seconds…

‘If I told you, would you agree not to disclose anything in writing or to the press, in any public or private way? And let me tell you, if you do, I know enough solicitors to make your life a misery should you not keep your promise.’

I pondered her threats for the sake of conveniences… Yet, she knew that I had no other choice but to accept her pact…

‘Do you want me to sign a confidentiality agreement?’ I said confidently undeterred.

‘What if I paid you a lump sum for your psychic investigation only if you could prove for certain that my father was innocent?’

‘Deal!’ I said unreservedly and too hastily in retrospect. I was a forlorn ascetic until I met Mrs Jones. Her 40-year walk through hell would stimulate my intellect and resuscitate my flagging spirit after Koroshiya’s departure. I could have kneeled and asked for her hand, had she not been fifty years older than me. But I was still a mere schmoozer with confused feelings… It remained Mrs Jones dispel any doubts about my missionary endeavours… Her ancestors were burnt at the stake, her heart had been bear-baited on the public square, her family name dragged in the mud of opprobrium… I couldn’t possibly understand how deep her scars ran and when I got home that day, I opened the Bible on Ezekiel, chapter 30 and read: "for with their mouth they show much love, but their hearts pursue their own gain".

So, what did the Hayfield village have to gain by accusing Private Jones of the murders? Was it going to start all over again with those fresh unsavoury discoveries on Kinder Scout? Who would be their next scapegoat?

The press was getting understandably impatient at the slow progress of the police. But how could they possibly find anything new in a 120-year-old case? What if the werewolf prankster was just part of a Halloween prank gone stale?

If Jones' exculpation had left an unsolved rancid serial murder case rumour floating in the old village, no one seemed to have any inclination to track a murderer who dressed his victims in Victorian clothes, let alone real Victorian bodies, which begged the following question: what if some village people were in on it?

I had to do some serious work to disentangle that mess, and with no relevant previous experience, my job was not cut and dried… The vainglorious and blusterous sermons of the well-to-do Revival evangelists did not hit home the following Sunday. I had to isolate again…

What are spirits made of? I pondered on Sunday afternoon after a bloating church service… The slight stomach discomfort I felt every time I became aware of a spirit calling, signalled the start of a paranormal incubation period… Sat in the armchair by the French door, looking at the neighbourhood green-eyed Manx cat, I felt my pulse quickening, my stomach heaving… It could be love, I wondered… That nervous feeling before the tempest of passion… But the butterflies were not as white or as colourful or even as exotic or majestic as love's signs…

What had Mrs Jones's father tried to tell me?

It's true that I had spotted a Romano girl selling the Big issue magazine in front of the Co-op. She had caught my eye as she willy-nilly tried selling her tabloids for £2.50. She was beautiful, yet dressed in a weird long black gypsy dress with an adorned silver bottom fringe, her hair dishevelled, and dark locks voluptuously framing her beautiful young olive complexion… I must have had a crush… I could be amorous or even desperate for love, while still in love with Koroshiya…

But this new stomach feeling meant something else … Those feelings weren't mine… Private Jones's wife was a gipsy. He had fallen in love and his unusual union with an outsider had cost him his standing in the community…

I had been sheepish with Mrs Jones. I was afraid to upset the apple cart and the opposite happened… She was in control. I had been kicked in the balls by the old guard of the Women's Institute running a Victorian lapse of honour around my miserable gifts. Yet, as I sat in my scratched and shabby-chic Ikea armchair, I knew it was another spirit calling… It couldn't be love.

◆◆◆

The most irreverent pastor Lucas Bean told me one day: 'Jesus Christ doesn't need followers or goody-two-shoes.'

We would meet for the Power Prayer at Church, at 8:30 am, on a Sunday morning… If I had had the presence of mind, I would have said to Mr Bean what I had on my chest about his silver-fingered attitude towards church finances… But I didn't. I only found out later… Christians are bound by the secrecy of corruption. What's more, if he didn't have those goody-two-shoes he referred to, there wouldn't be any volunteers doing the hard work for him…

Mr Bean also spoke in tongues, although there was no revulsion of eyes, no wobbling of the knees at a seismic level big enough to move mountains, except perhaps a few ripples in muffin tops. It remains the pantomime was fun enough for a while… What's more, there were one or two people worth knowing…

I am ever so grateful to the Holy Spirit for showing me how this Broadway of Faith had its limit, even in entertainment terms.

Mrs Jones was incredibly open-minded and humorous about the whole affair when I contacted her to expose my plan, and she even encouraged me to find out more about her 'genus'. But her tolerance for the supernatural was limited…

With her help, her family tree on her father's side could be traced back to Russian immigrants, as it stood… There was right there a stigma one could not disregard… I didn't need genomics to know Mrs Jones was an Ashkenazi Jew… Eastern Europe had brought anarchists and communists alike, and among them spies associated with the nobility. It was hard to tell who fled Russia first and to which social class Mrs Jones' ancestors belonged. Then again, the name Jones suggested Welsh heritage… So, I could not straight away ascertain which class Mrs Jones' ascendants belonged to without her help. What I learned was that the Russian nobility left an enormous wake of destruction and mayhem after their passage to the West…

Born an immigrant myself, I could relate to Mrs Jones chaotic history… But who couldn't, especially in England where 80% of the population are the descendants of an invader?

The name Jones was the result of a naturalisation process started by Private Jones' father. But things didn't turn out as well as they should have, once Mr Jones senior became British… Just like the anarchist Bakunin, Jones senior had made his way to England in the 1860s. Private Jones was born in 1890. More or less, the same year as his spirit had said. His father had a cabinet-making business which seemed to thrive until 1894 and the Great Depression, when, from the odorous social compost of industrialisation, emerged vigilantes like Jack the Ripper whose terrible acts book-ended the price depression in England.

What happened to Jones senior during those years of public penury and private ostentation? Was Private Jones scarred by a miserable childhood? I needed to know more to brush a more complete portrait of a possible fiend who would have known the Joneses personally… Mrs Jones would provide me with the missing pieces of the puzzle…

'Why do you need so much fact, if you're a psychic?' asked Mrs Jones point-blank as I stood at her doorstep, the following Saturday…

But after reading those excerpts from the census in Mrs Jones study, during the month of August, I began to see how the 19th century might connect to the modern disappearances…

Villagers rarely look among the well-established family trees to find evil, yet it's the genesis of established power that breeds the most brutal truth. Among the landowners and gentry, there are secrets untold even to the modern generations who have been shaped after their fashion and by their standards…

I explained to Mrs Jones how in my own private history, an illegitimate relationship between a count and his servant brought about our family name and our doom…

'Why doom?' enquired Mrs Jones… laying the table for our now weekly session…

'Well… I believe it's been a curse and I think I know why…'

'A curse, really?'

'I think it is…' I said seriously. 'You see… Many of my relatives, on my mother's side, died unexpectedly, whether from disease or sudden accidental death… And I mean many… Right to this day, I can't remember any of them to be alive… And guess what… I am probably the only one to know why…'

'I mean is it doom or destiny?' asked Mrs Jones portentously.

'I am still unsure…'

'Which is a good sign… Let's start,' she said smiling quizzically.

I told Mrs Jones how the information I held on her family could come handy in a salon conversation too… Rumours were often randomly spread like breadcrumbs by busybodies.

The Jones' family was a sociological construct of the industrial era and the village had given their dog a bad name and hanged it. The libellous campaign against the immigrant family took no prisoners. But to protect whom? It was time to ask Mrs Jones if she was ready for an evocation with her ancestors…

‘So let’s start, Mrs Jones, shall we?’ I said laying my hands on the German oak table.

‘Spirits, spirits…’ said Mrs Jones, shaking with anticipation.

‘Please, Mrs Jones…’ I interrupted. ‘This is not how it works… You need a guide… You can’t invoke spirits out of the blue…’

‘Why not!’ exclaimed Mrs Jones.

‘I will start by asking you a few questions… Just answer them… When we get to the 26th question, I will give you a sign and this will put you in a trance-like state… From there, I will recall your true family history…’

Mrs Jones nodded dubitatively…

‘26?’

‘26.’

Once challenged, she would be open to guile or so I thought although it wasn’t my intention to trump her… In case anyone wonders what being a psychic is all about… This is it. It’s about letting the subject dot the lines; it’s all about suggestion…

I would learn later nothing ever happened by chance… It usually takes disbelief to get started and get hooked in… The heart is filled with doubts, graves and impatience.

◆◆◆

Planets in our solar system move in a pigtail fashion through space and are never still or at the same location in space. This is how time works… We wouldn’t have time if the solar system didn’t move forward… We advance in time, yet our memories never leave us… Indeed, how is it possible that we should remember them? Surely, the brain is not isolated in this time continuum… Somehow, when we recall memories, we are able to connect to those ribbons of time torn from our flesh. But it is not our brain's work, if it were, our memory would be blank and uncontrollable, and no sooner lived than erased… We would only remember what we have just been living… Talking of which, I remember this conversation I had with Koroshiya in the church café one day… Koroshiya refused to go to church at first… She didn't want to be evangelised.

'I don't really want to get too abstract this morning, but I think our body doesn't really allow for a relationship with space other than feeling the effect of gravity or the pool of the moon…'

'Precisely,' I said, 'what if we could have a deeper understanding of our flesh as space travellers? I mean, you're a scientist, how would you go about laying down some math or theorems for this?'

'What do you mean? It's a spiritual quest, I guess…'

Before I walked towards Mrs Jones' house for the last time, I made a detour by my garden, the property of the 19th century protestant lady who devoted her life to teetotalism.

I had heard a branch from her garden knocking on the outside ridge of my slate roof. Of course, it wasn't hers any longer… In fact, all houses down the embankment which stood behind my house were now rented out. The culprit tuned out to be a beech tree branch which I had to saw in half with a thought for the old lady and the Bargain Booze shop I could see from the embankment…

Walking on the Sett Valley trail to Hayfield before meeting Mrs Jones, I rehashed my theory on the time-space continuum… I looked behind me trying to recall wilfully and consciously what I had seen a few minutes back on the trail: a couple walking hand in hand in summery clothes, smiling at me and saying hello with the mawkish magnanimity of a couple obviously in love… I hadn't seen the man's face but had seen hers clearly… She looked ordinary. But I remembered clearly their natural happy demeanour. This was Koroshiya and I before the house took hold of us.

What had happened exactly? Was our love so weak that it couldn't conquer death? What if instead of moving forward, the universe was moving backwards in time? On a philosophical level, this would change our conception of good and bad as death is no longer an end in itself, but a necessary beginning… Given the future is already known, whereas we spend countless hours thinking about it, wouldn't we waste less time in trying to predict it or influence it, if time moved backwards?

It would give us more time to live our lives too… Then, we would not need explain why we are dust and return to dust since dust is beneath our feet and behind us. Then, for every dawn God makes, it would just be a day closer to the day of creation, not the last… I could remember a dog wobbling erratically with a spring in its step into the undergrowth and in and out of the path… I could remember the signs to the bluebell wood and the local species of birds and plants… Yet, I knew for certain that those memories would soon fade as many meaningless fleeting moments, as I walked deeper into the woods and the winding trail towards Mrs Jones' house… I knew that much. I was reassured thinking my little journey on the trail had its place in space-time too, if only for a brief moment…

I then realised that emotions are what make us remember episodes of our life forever, as they carve their outlines in our soul… As I mused how these 'carving' moments could have a place in space, and be shared any way other than by language, from one human to another, I opened the last gate on the Sett valley trail to enter Hayfield…

It had taken me an hour to walk to Mrs Jones's house. I rang the bell. She opened the door… I apologised for my muddy boots which we agreed were to be blamed on last night's heavy rains and my recent intolerance to chores… Her face was amenable yet soberly brooding… She was dressed in black. She wanted to look the part, I guess…

Mrs Jones had laid the table with her special afternoon tea crockery. I noticed how pale she had become in the lounge mirror:

'Mrs Jones, spirits can take hold of the ones you love, and it makes me angry,' I said to her mirrored reflexion. Mrs Jones turned around and opened the door to the garden…

'It's a nice day, isn't it?'

'It is, Mrs Jones, without a doubt.'

Her family pictures were displayed on the mantelpiece and the chest of drawers… She visibly had planned for her paranormal session tonight… There was a slight smell of wax in the room where I followed her sheepishly, striding across enormous limestone slabs. The smell of wax originated from her aged kitchen pine furniture… There was a china cabinet along with a huge pine Danish dresser decorated with hand crafted yellow plates and mugs…

Although her garden was in bloom, I found it odd that there shouldn't be any flower vase in any of the downstairs room. But a corny cat with a velvety maroon fur stepped in with the mid-afternoon breeze to distract us both in our musings…

Before long, Mrs Jones sat at the table and asked me to join her, a picture frame in her left hand. It seemed as though she was trying to read it with her fingers and with a slightly uncanny smile on her face… We started talking about Kinder Scout…

'I want to know how he died, that's all I want to know.'

'Your mother never told you? Of course, you were too small. Maybe a parent? Why do you think there could have been foul play?' I said looking into her piercing eyes as they shone like two valiant stars in the middle of her emaciated façade… I began feeling odd, beside myself, as in a trance…

'I know he died here in this house which belonged to him, but my mother wouldn't say… Or anyone else, for that matter… It's a family secret and that's why you're here.'

◆◆◆

'You damned bitch!'

'Mrs Jones, who is a bitch, is that you, Jones?'

'She is…'

There was a slight blockage on the part of Mrs Jones. It had taken me two hours to get there… It would take me two hours back… I could always fill in the blanks later… But I was afraid Mrs Jones might be hurt in the process… So, I backtracked by steering the session back to her time…

She fumbled for those space-time memories of infant and toddler years to tell me she remembered her dad as a small child… Soon, the first lights of day started colouring the horizon… One could see the vegetation taking shape against the morning sky…

'He was a man of his time, I guess. He always wore those baggy dungarees with a sleeveless T-shirt. Those are my summer memories of him… I remember his hair was always placated and combed backward in a wavy pattern. He used an old brand of colloidal gel called Gomina all the time… I still remember the comb he held in his back pocket and the hair on its teeth… He had a gentle voice but breathed with difficulty. At times, he was panting for breath. My mother told me he was at the Somme, where he was made prisoner. He could speak German.'

The sun shining through the dappled windowpanes had lulled us into a time warp…

'I remember his dad's name was Gunter, that was also the name of my great grandfather…'

'So, why did his parents emigrate from Germany?' I asked. She was now holding her granddaughter's portrait.

'He had to kill his bitch once.'

'I beg your pardon?'

'He killed his own dog with a club… That's the only time I was ever afraid in his presence… He resented his dog being sick of course. But somehow, we all knew he had rather kill his sick bitch than let her suffer. He was tough.'

'I can't imagine what it must have been like to be a prisoner of the Bosch… Mrs Jones, I really met your pa… On Kinder… I recognise him now…' I said cursorily.

'Oh Dad…'

'Mrs Jones. Could it be that he died there?'

'No…' said Mrs Jones categorically.

‘I read in the newspapers that he fled when his wife was discovered… He had to hide there for a while… They hounded him like a dog for the murder of my ma. But he died in his own house, of that I’m sure.’

Mrs Jones told the whole story she had been told by her mother… She didn’t want to hear the truth. If he had died in his own house, there wouldn’t be any mystery to his death. Elucidating questions until the following sunset, Mrs Jones showed no sign of letting go. How he returned from the war and married a gypsy, her mother… How they taunted him about it, in the village. How her mother had looked into her own past for clues and shared her advice with her own daughter… She remembered in her mother’s voice how the hunt for her father had stigmatised her, like his imprisonment, his release several months later due to new evidence. How the unsolved murder was related in the condemning and parochial press, how girls at school had defiled her father’s memory once they got wind of her family history, how her own parents had to move to Manchester, how she became a seamstress using her mother’s maiden name, Walker… She remembered it all as if her mother’s tale had been told yesterday. Her mother Mary Ann was a woman of extreme beauty, she recalled. She married three times, the second time to a Manchester man whom late Mrs Jones never loved, and the third time, into a wealthy Derbyshire family, a local lawyer. She was an only child…

Her pain was so vivid that it was hard to believe she only knew her family’s history through her mother’s account. But Mrs Jones was desperate to know how her father’s soul could be put at rest, and that was why she was willing to talk to me… I could now follow the signs of time on her face, her slightly olive wrinkles were like the very precious skin of a rare book cover, like many rivulets leading into the meaning of her soul…

'I want to know if he died in peace with himself…' she said after a break.

'We'll find out soon enough, Mrs Jones… Soon enough,' I said before parting with her for a few hours' errand. Mrs Jones' account had brought nostalgic spasms in my stomach. Our families are far from being picture-perfect. Somehow, I had forgotten that the blue-eyed waitress at Millie's had told me a few days before that Mrs Jones was a guest there… Why did Mrs Jones stay there? Drilled by this nagging thought, I walked towards Millie's again, firmly decided to clear this odd fact before tonight's session, but the café was closed… For that matter, apart from a smoky fish and chip shop, the main street was deserted. I noticed it was Sunday night on my phone. The bells of St Matthew rang seven… I walked past a stream spewing out of the hill near the Old Hall Hotel and stopped at the WWI memorial to the unknown soldier once again… Walking into the Old Hall Hotel and pub, I ordered a cheeseburger and a decaf coffee. It felt nearly indecent to have doubts about a client and her reasons for wanting to communicate with her dead loved ones. But Mrs Jones was still hiding part of the truth…

Back at Mrs Jones' house, I laid down my professional paraphernalia on the floor… I had managed to pop at my house for a shower and to pick up some equipment. I don't call myself a medium, as the medium concept is ultimately a fallacy. I merely facilitate communication with the other side thanks to my gifts. But I had to warn Mrs Jones that this was my last session ever with her.

Somehow, I had to give her an ultimatum. If it didn't create the desired effect, at least it would make her reach her chequebook… Not that I had never talked to spirits before, but calling one out had never happened to me. So, I started with an orthodox prayer for the dead… 'Lead me back again to thy likeness, refashioning my ancient beauty.'

I looked around the house to see a reaction and among the family portraits for a clue. Nothing… Mrs Jones opened one eye and closed it again hurriedly.

'I would like to get down to it, if you'll allow me, Mrs Jones.'

'Let me take the picture of my father, here it is…' she said, methodically…

Something happened straight away… I was chased by a spirit… Mrs Jones turned around and snatched the picture of her father and his wife. A trail of images first assaulted me. Their life had been bloody and violent. Trains… Modernity… Mechanical demons, urban jungles… Lost souls… A pair of gloves…

'We're in the midst of the industrial revolution…' I said, panting for effect. Part of my brain was conscious still, conscious that Mrs Jones should see what was going on… But suddenly, I heard – I felt rather, as tactile as sand, the waves that came to me, which my brain analysed as human – people coughed; spat the dirt of their lungs on the pavement. Every second was an agonising struggle and a mad attempt at survival. I was on a train… I heard the rattling of the beams and carriage wheels and a drowsy series of numbers came to me… I felt a woman's breasts under a green duffel coat… She felt as a fading rose… Then came tubular voices and sounds… I felt hands on mine. I felt the vibrations passing through her body as well as mine, but the images were too opaque. I wasn't able to see the real world beyond…

'Who are you?'

'I don't know… It was about time someone told me…' said a man humorously.

I heard a deep masculine voice close to me, close to my chest… My mind was busy with the practicalities of a trip to the seaside…

'A blessing in disguise,' she thought.

I was in her gipsy soul castle. She thought of a bird pissing on the streets. How queer… She felt their gaze. She was listening to mothers shouting with anguish at their children to warn them of the dangers around them. She felt barren… I was still conscious myself, and I could hear my thoughts reverberating in some tunnel of the time-space continuum. I supposed Private Jones was sitting opposite her. It was their first holidays. Life was a gift, God was omnipresent.

'Where are you my darling?'

'Who told you I was gone? I came back, didn't I?'

'You were hurt. They killed you…'

'No, I did it to myself…'

'Why? Didn't I make you happy?'

'I couldn't take their gaze anymore… They killed me with their condemning eyes…'

The man felt suddenly alone, and I assumed was talking to the ghost of a memory. I suddenly felt Mrs Jones pressing her hand on mine. It was a kind, comforting gesture. I opened my eyes. The sun had risen. I was safe…

'I had a duffel coat, once,' I said to Mrs Jones, leaning on her cottage pine kitchen as she was frying some bacon… It was a detail that woke me up to the here and now…

'Oh, did you now?'

'Yes, I was a kid. I used to love the little hoops and wooden buttons… I loved going to school with it, in winter.'

'So how did you become a psychic?' she said. I noticed her hands were shaking…

'Some have greatness thrown upon them, some achieve greatness,' I said, quoting Shakespeare.

'What you said last night… about her was striking…'

'What was that Mrs Jones?' I would seldom remember my psychic lucubration after the deed. Mrs Jones must have been unknowingly shocked, but she was a strong woman…

'How she lived in the eyes of others…'

I suppose I was drained out of my senses as I couldn't remember falling asleep in Mrs Jones' garden while she popped out for some eggs… But it's when I woke up the nose in her rose bush that I realised I'd slept on a bench on a wet patch of lawn. How I'd come to sleep, and first of all, in her garden, I would only find out when she would come back… As I opened my eyes, I could see Mrs Jones's orange tea rose bush standing triumphantly nascent behind a corner stone, on the second terrace…

Multi-tiered gardens are frequent in the Peak where houses are flanked against knolls or hills. I noticed a conspicuous plum tree and an apple tree kissing each other over a makeshift wattle fence extending uphill, while over an elevated terrace, a table, two chairs and a weathered bench were laid out to face the afternoon sun on the third level. An erected grey moss-ridden slab, probably used as a makeshift fence, attracted my attention besides the two trees exchanging curtsies over the fence. It looked strangely like a tombstone…

The birds were singing the day's praise and flying in the glowing sunset…

When I turned around to get up, I saw two skulls beside me and quickly got to my feet. There at arm's reach, I could see two cats' skulls polished into little dainty alabaster sculptures by the elements. As I turned around to wake up, a cuddly maroon cat stroked my leg.

I looked at its whiskers while the affectionate cat rubbed against my thigh… I would have sworn it was speaking.

◆◆◆

No one knew her…

'Are you sure?'

'But the blue-eyed girl you talked to could be anyone of our staff and no, Mrs Jones is not one of our guests anymore… She died ten years ago!'

'Who the fuck have I been spoken to these last few days then?' I eructed, pining on the dark wooden floor of Millie's Café like a bull. I was told to mind my language…

'What? How come you heard what I've just said? I mean… I'm surprised because no one ever hears anything around here! I spoke to Mrs Jones only a few hours ago…'

I left without slamming the door as it was open. It was then I realised I had been played. I waved… But I was right. Mrs Jones had been dead ten years. And yet, someone, at the pub, had also directed me to Millie's and then from Millie's to her house… It was incomprehensible. I remembered the card in my back pocket. Was it still there? What about the Women's Institute?

I now suspected the village to have staged a Cluedo play where I was a mere stooge. I was a school kid prank away from committing a horrible murder just to give those damn facetious inbreds a run for their money. But I bottled in and decided I should return home to ease my nerves. I searched but couldn't find any trace of the card… The house itself was inhabited by a couple with a baby. I simply could not see how I had been deadlocked into a pantomime staged by spirits…

But after I calmed down, walking back home, I realised how this could only mean one thing… I was on to the truth about the Joneses. I had dug up a few skeletons hidden in the picturesque closets of Hayfield… And spirits had played a trick on me.

By 6 am, the next day, I had prepared all my equipment, my EMF, EDI, IR kit and cameras, determined to find Mrs Jones out… If she had been expecting me and staged a farce, I wouldn't be blamed for not making a last-ditch effort. I owed it to Jones and his memory… He had the right to know why he died…

On my way to Kinder Scout, all that happened on the Peak Mountain and in the village reeled back like a kaleidoscope… Jones died peacefully, but how peacefully exactly? This didn't fit with the irate and inane rambling of the man I met on the cold windy summer night around the atavistic fire… I was lost. I had to give up, but I couldn't. I came up with another ridiculous idea: What if the body of the Victorian woman food on the mountain was Mrs Jones?

The Outer Path

Whatever the story of Mrs Jones was all about; it had remained untold until I investigated a seemingly unrelated series of murders. It could have been my story; it could have been anyone else's. Where do we go when our spirit dies? Do we live on? Do spirits join the ranks of a dead army? Or are they loaned to us for a lifetime and then returned to their lender? Are we not just death's trustees? By the time Mrs Jones left the picture, I was roaming the streets trying to cross gazes with strangers, believing I was a hollow man in need of fuelling up with soul matter.

We all strive to transcend our bodily limitations. Athletes, scientists, even politicians, when they lie beyond their reach. But my call was otherness… Speaking of which, who was the woman I met if she wasn't Mrs Jones? Who cared… I would never find out anyway… This is what happened to amateur psychics… I had more pressing matters at hand… For example, what about the air of depression about town? It wasn't just Koroshiya and I, but the whole town which seemed despondent… Living looked like a compulsory exercise. Smiling it seemed, was frowned upon. I wouldn't say it was prohibited, because they were no laws against it, but smiling for pleasure without selling anything was out of the question here… At least, not on the streets…

Where should I start again? I thought… How to investigate such an intangible concept as smile prohibition? How did it work exactly? Were zygomatic muscles any worse than sphincters? Yet, assholes couldn't stop venting out their miserable odorous platitudes around the popular places… Cafes, takeaways, pubs… No one laughed heartedly, no one smiled but under the sordid forceful drive of a conventional necessity… Or when they did, they had to justify why they smiled or make sure there was a reason behind it for fear of being caught red-handed in the act of smiling out of happiness… Otherness as a hole to be filled…

Gravity certainly played a huge part in the fact the use of zygomatic muscles was rationed. Indeed, from a physical point of view, jaws tend to drop naturally, whereas it takes much effort to pick up a smile from where it's lying, six feet under a blanket of crass and self-interest… Inventors never even bothered inventing smart helium balloons to lift up those zygos out of their slumber for a reason… It would never have sold. It would have been regarded as redundant, leading to self-harm, or simply eccentric. When you study a species, you have to look at the most significant specimen. The queen… Now, the Queen of England grins and notoriously so. Anyone can see it's a devil's job to make the queen smile, as she is already under a lot of pressure to just be there… Even taking this into account, one can occasionally espy the Queen Elizabeth flashing her royal fangs with ingenuity for a split second, which is sadly too short to qualify as a trend-setting fashion statement… Indeed, pompous ceremonies are notoriously laden with gravitas and serosity. There is no question that that the same argument can be turned on its head. It can be said, conversely, that the queen smiles to please her people and has adopted the national grin to remain popular… Sadly, the queen smiles… But is it to show favour or to elucidate compassion? Yet, in those rare moments when her subjects show a genuine interest in happiness, the queen just bows to circumstances and nods assent with a yet another constricted grin.

I had begun noticing lately how the reverse droop was the commonest of all tentative smiles in my town of residence… I had started my investigation into the act of smiling without knowing it… Suddenly, I caught a glimpse of my reflection passing the charity shop window and I saw it. It was there in display… It did not surprise the woman in charge of revamping the window for the old people's charity and who just managed to evade such an antagonistic situation that may arise between two strangers smiling at each other…

'Aye! Hope is the killer!' I said to the shop manager…

'A little dance, maybe?' I mimed through the window, suggesting she should wriggle along with me… which she did gladly. *How cute,* I thought…

Soon winter came with its low-profile evenings and damp and cold slashings. We hadn't heard from the Kinder Scout killer in a while… As a matter of fact, a few months had passed since my "encounter" with the Joneses. And everyone avoided the subject for fear of opening old wounds… The mood was getting geared towards Christmas lights, not Victorian corpses… At the church café, I met Julian:

'How have you been?' she said, on an engaging tone…

'Fine…' I said simply.

I never really expanded on the details of my mood even with long time acquaintances… Julian had bipolar disorder. That's how the celebrated post WWII health system had revolutionised Europe to describe what being a woman felt like… It's interesting how planetary this phenomenon had become, yet I'd never seen it in the flesh, except here, the home of pharmaceutical genius.

By the time Mrs Jones came out of the picture; I was reduced to roaming the streets of Manchester only avoiding archetypal jugglers with a silly grin on their face… In front of the shop window, I felt my bipolar lesbian friend was hitting on me… Why? She was just selling her merchandise and doing it with the eagerness that characterises women at work!

'The bibulous brothers have done it again,' I commented on the news, once I found a seat at the church café where Julian's girlfriend came to order her mid-morning latte…

The in-out referendum results were a clear split in the middle, save for a mere million and two hundred voices that had tilted the balance towards Brexit. It could be said that this number amounted approximately to the number of immigrants who had fled from Syria, I argued to an imaginary interlocutor who had yet to flesh out among the customers… The bibulous brothers had both European ascendancies. One was the descendant of a German prince, once a governor of Finland, and the other, of Huguenot lineage and German heritage. *How queer,* I thought… Then I remembered how much American capital transited through Britain where 50 % of the GDP was created by foreign-owned companies… It all made sense… Somehow, a suite of murky self-anointed renegades had pursued their own self-enrichment to the detriment of democracy… Of course, for good measure, once the Machiavellian order was restored, those two free-thinking mavericks would levy their commission for services rendered to history… Julian brought me a smoky cappuccino… Nothing would change for the better as the only capital to be squandered on British ground would come from the US anyway, since the rest of investors would relocate to Europe and the new financial centres…

Julian always forgot I took brown sugar with my coffee… Once I had finished reading the press, I felt uneasy… It was a victory for the people who hadn't a clue… They had been swayed by a clear political agenda, yet couldn't see the wood for the trees, namely politics unloading their foul semen of vengeful dissent without a care in the world for consequences… On the other hand, the gravy HS2 train was being brought up to speed…

Nothing patriotic in washing your ancestral dirty linen in public, I thought, *and I should know…*

'What are you on about?' said Julian.

'Nothing,' I said sipping my coffee and throwing the Times in anger… I was still recriminating about the Joneses. The papers landed on the floor and Julian picked it up. We were already going through a financial meltdown, that's all. Why not commit suicide on top? Inject more dollars into the economy and live as slaves for the rest of our lives just because the short-sighted progeny of stateless migrants wanted to vent out their grudge against the society that never really recognised them as their own?

'Nothing… Actually, I'll take my coffee near the window… I need some light…'

I had heard enough about divorce, and I knew how hurtful old couples can be when they take advantage of the other's weakness. I had been there before… There is no such thing as an amicable divorce. I also knew how the rest of the European block would do anything in their power to make Brexit a personal matter too. It was clear that the Conservative and right-wing politicians had a hollow point to make, and just like the financial crisis had been triggered by big banks to help governments take back control over the inventive and truly revolutionary financial world, those two spearheads of capitalism were in fact regents of an old bipolar schism between the richest and the poorest. It was all obvious: The Victorian-inherited cesspits of poverty versus exuberant lavish orgies, East versus West London, or the establishment versus parliamentarianism model they were emulating, the very retrograde model of society the industrial revolution was based upon, where the monarch was the centre of the world…

Once again, the so-called liberals had fallen for the personality cult.

'See those two, that lacking foppish caricature of a gentry squire and him, that hyperventilating schoolboy…' I said to Dylan, the manager of the church café…

'They got there by pushing the right buttons: vanity… That's how people vote… What they can't afford is vanity… When you think about it, those puppet-masters knew where to pull…'

'Not that I care, of course, as the Western world is going down anyway… I just wish they would make up their mind…'

'This is Zechariah to the letter…' said Dylan, quoting the Bible:

'On that day his feet will stand on the Mount of Olives, east of Jerusalem, and the Mount of Olives will be split in two from east to west, forming a great valley…'

‘Sure,’ said Dylan. ‘They don’t know where they’re going… They’re loose cannons.’

In my line of trade, the papers are what grounds you to reality. Although, I must admit that sometimes the version of events you are presented in the Times is quite surreal. It was the blissful end of summer 2016. Koroshiya and I had been divorced for four years. I was contemplating putting a noose around my neck to hang my body from a tree on a countryside road, just above the middle of the road discontinuous line…

Then again, I might become gay to see the world differently, as an out-of-body experience exercise…

Instead, I decided to train as a vicar.

Absolution

Thank God, Halloween was over… I had waited all summer for winter to come, so I could resume my diary of psychic investigations. Some overzealous traditionalists had cracked fireworks until the early hours of the morning to celebrate Guy Fawkes' failed Gun Powder plot and the safety of James I.

I simply resented the fact that Halloween and bonfire night always contrived to expedite the Christmas countdown, and it is in that jolly spirit, on Monday, 6th of November 2025—my head feeling like a pumpkin—that I was directed to Mike Crompton's office in West Didsbury.

It had been raining all night continuously… The glittering pavements had a knife-edge, metallic stillness that alerted your senses to the cold, nearly invisible drizzle. And it was a cold day by any standard.

Mike had been detached temporarily from Newton Heath to oversee a task force that had been set up as part of a widespread operation to investigate acid attacks that plagued the wealthy South Manchester neighbourhood. He had requested my presence with insistence.

The stocky fellow's fiery ginger sideburns were the first detail I noted about him. I had put on my usual Panglossian facade, but a dark motive behind his call had me cautious…

'Good morning, reverend, pleased to meet you!'

The gingerbread man's pleasantries sounded sweet, but I remained attentive.

'Just call me Jupiter,' I said, auspiciously conscious I was meeting the maverick who had booted Andrew out of the investigation into the Kinder Scout murders.

'So, Jupiter, I just wanted to thank you for your help on the Kinder Scout murders on behalf of the whole department. How long ago was it, seven years? I know Andrew Cunningham is your acolyte now. You two make a great team, although I'm not sure about your methods. This is why we are here, really… By the way, a "collective hallucination", is that right?'

Now I could see why his beady Irish eyeballs were shining with malice. He was referring to my book… I had published my account of my investigation and the police were not happy that I had exposed their miserable failings in the case.

'I am not entirely sure what you mean, but apart from the Victorian bodies in question, which were a hoax, the rest was entirely true and my account of the investigation will not be published as agreed with your services.'

A group of malfeasant farmers had found the preserved mummified body of one of Jack the Ripper's victims, Ann Mary Nichols, who towards 1889 was sold on the morbid black market against solid gold to a Liverpudlian collector who later settled in the High Peak, taking his macabre memorabilia with him. The body had been found in a grave on one of their lands and they somehow decided their village needed a boost in tourism.

'But were there not two bodies, Jupiter?'

'Yes, the second one, which was never identified, was that of Mrs Jones, I assume…'

'Bone-chilling…'

'Indeed…'

'And what about the two 'modern' women who actually disappeared from the village?'

Mike Crompton's constricted smirk belied his placid sleuthing, but I held firm…

'Two lesbians who had indeed done a runner… That rumour was true… Even, the most acute police work couldn't have anticipated that,' I claimed, as I felt a damp patch on the padded office chair, having disregarded his head gesture pointing towards the coat hanger on the mat white office door.

He slowly opened a grey cardboard folder, feigning institutionalised suspense:

'You didn't wet your cassock for nothing, reverend.' He smirked offhandedly.

'Am I wearing a cassock, Mr Crompton?'

'Sorry. It seemed like a good joke at the time… Can't blame me for trying…' he said with a sneering chuckle.

'I am following an important lead in the case of Sir Tony's wife, and I will be asking for your cooperation. It's a new case. That's why I thought I was here,' I said forcefully, nipping his humorous jives in the bud. I was decidedly not in the mood for religious banter.

'A lead? Oh, that's right, Sir Tony has asked you to apply your "talents" to further his case, hasn't he now?'

'Not yet, but I have good hopes he will soon…'

Policemen enjoy dishing out mundanities while stabbing you in the back in the same breath; a vocational bias. I was facing a veteran, no doubt about that…

'So, you want me to allow you to question witnesses in a cold case, I presume? You know the case was closed eight years ago, right? By the way, we have had a complaint from George Calvin, Irving's cousin, already. To use his words, you ruffled his son's feathers! That's how I know you've started investigating without authorisation.'

'It's not exactly true. I asked him a few questions about Sir Tony's alibi. It's not the last time either. I intend to interview him again, with the assistance of Andrew Cunningham, with your permission.'

He rolled his eyes disrespectfully at the sound of Andrew's name. I decided I couldn't sing along to his Irish tune, even if he sprung to his feet and started a facetious Trenchmore.

'Will you stop interrogating witnesses on the police's behalf for now? What's more, Andrew is not in charge, I am! Oh, and MacCloskey, I don't like arresting vicars, so please, stay away from this case until you have had the official green light.'

'I beg your… Mike, I can assure you my intentions are pure… I can do this. I was born to solve crimes… You know I am…' I said ingenuously.

'Indeed, all credit due to you, Reverend.'

'I'll be discrete.'

I was proud of my record and rightfully so. Andrew could testify in my favour… Well, maybe not just now… But Sir Tony needed help with the murder of his wife and that was binding enough to me.

'Very well… If you're a psychic, why don't you solve the Ripper case, while we're at it, and if you do, I will let you carry on with your investigation into Sir Tony's wife's death…'

He paused a moment, eager to catch some expression of disconcertment on my face.

'The ripper case from the Victorian era? Very well…'

'I'd like to know how you follow evidence. I can even pledge unfettered access to Helena Irving's murder case files if you convince me. I just need to know you can investigate… professionally, I mean.'

Report to Mike Crompton

In 1888, while the London East End slums were being earmarked for demolition, Jack the Ripper did the dirty work for property developers who had their eyes set on the last-standing rookeries of Whitechapel and Spitalfields. Crime was rife and living conditions miserly. Ganged-up riff-raffs terrorised prostitutes and lodgers, in what seemed to be a deterrent to the Jewish settlements and an attempt at thwarting the already well underway cheap land grab of the Four Percent Industrial Dwelling Company set up by Baron Rothschild, in Flower and Dean Street, Spitalfields.

Two plaques commemorating Robert Horner's rebuilding of the Spitalfields market are still visible today. The former market porter had bought a short seventy-year lease and became a private owner of the Spitalfields Market. He completed the rebuilding at a cost of £80,000.

It is reasonable to assume that a market porter might have needed financial help and therefore wasn't the only person involved in the development. A small commemorating plaque on Lam Street actually indicates that Robert Horner "finished" rebuilding the market in 1893. The workforce needed to build the sprawling suburb attracted immigrants and outsiders from all over Europe. They took up lodgings to serve the Londonians' growing labour needs, while in the area of Wentworth, the rented Modern Model Dwellings financed by Rothschild provided accommodation for Jewish traders who dealt in second-hand clothes or footwear.

Among the throng of "unfortunates" who had gathered to celebrate the Golden Jubilee of Queen Victoria, on the 20th of June 1887, an organised handful of pimps and mercenaries began a cruel cat-herding hunt that still baffles the Metropolitan Police to this day.

The Gory Folklore

Catherine Eddowes and Elizabeth Stride's bodies were found on the 30th of September. Annie Chapman's had been found 27 days before, on September 8th and Mary Ann Nichols's on August 31st, 1888.

At 2:45 am, in a doorway of the Wentworth Model Dwellings, PC Alfred Long discovered a piece of Catherine Kate Eddowes' leather apron. She was the second prostitute murdered in the early hours of Sunday, 30th September 1888 in what is known as the "double event".

The apron presented bloody finger marks and the trace of a knife blade wiped clean.

The body of Catherine Eddowes was found five days after the "Dear Boss" letter was sent to the Central News Agency, prompting the Police of White Chapel to take the letters seriously and recognise it as the Ripper's.

The Ripper had promised to clip the victim's earlobes in his facetious letter dated 25th of September and did just that to Catherine Eddowes. The author of the red ink letter also strangely referred to a ginger bottle containing blood and used as a pen pot, as if to redound the German legend of Faust where the conjuror makes a pact with the devil by signing his immortal indenture with his own blood.

The "Dear Boss" Ripper letter and post-card

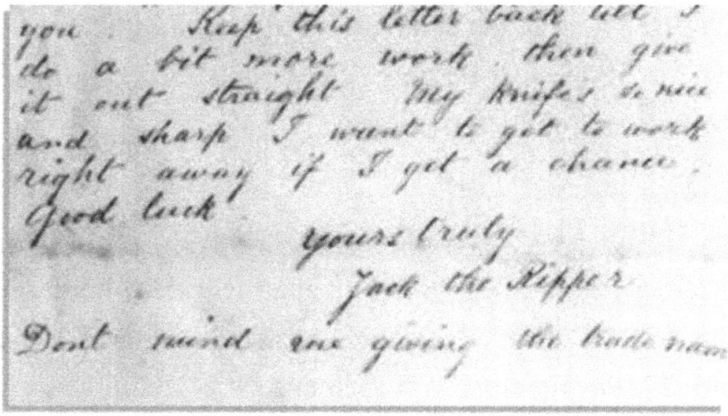
you. Keep this letter back till I
do a bit more work, then give
it out straight. My knife's so nice
and sharp I want to get to work
right away if I get a chance.
Good luck.
yours truly
Jack the Ripper
Dont mind me giving the trade nam

The date of the 25th of September is on the right-hand side, which indicates knowledge of letter heading practices and propriety. The forward-slanted handwriting indicates a need for sentiment or approbation and respect for form and conventions, and generally the mother figure. The grammar indicates good literacy and good writing skills for the period and the graphology reveals an eagerness to please and embellish.

The punctuation, namely the full stops, indicates both haste and hesitation, consistent with a professional reflective individual, which could also be attributed to a writing offset posture where the writing paper would be far to the right of the pen holder, but the handwriting is otherwise flowing and steady. There are instances where the punctuation and the register suggest a lower-class background or manner of speech. Expressions such as “won’t fix me just yet”, “get buckled”, “proper” are all meant to give a cocky and brash turn to the letter, but the handwriting and the use of accurate grammar dispel this pretence.

The letter was received by the Central News Agency on the 27th. If, as some reports suggest, the letter had been written by a journalist to create a sensational hype around the case, it understandably would have aimed to put the trickster’s newspaper on the map, rather than sent directly to the Central News Agency.

However, the far-right position of the writing paper may suggest the immediate space in front of the writer was unavailable due to the presence of a typewriter – hence the disjointed full stops at the end of each sentence, but the full stops after a sentence may also indicate reserve, construction and deceit, as if to impersonate a working-class author. This reserve or hesitation before a new sentence is highly pronounced in the Ripper’s letter, indicating reflexive pauses and painstaking composition…

Given that the blood-smeared saucy jack postcard which followed the “double event” was written in the same vein and handwriting, there are sufficient grounds to treat this body of evidence jointly with the “Dear Boss” letter.

The “saucy jack” postcard smeared with blood and sent to the Central News Agency bears a postmark dated 1st October 1888 and refers to the two murders committed during the weekend. In both letters, the slant to the right is not excessive, which tells us the writer is relatively balanced, which suggests the author was not the savage, unorganised ripper himself, but a methodical person. I have disregarded the “letter from Hell” as it’s not the same handwriting. If anything, the partial human kidney sent with this letter may serve to corroborate the practice of trading human organs on the black market for the purpose of medical research.

Meanwhile, the body of evidence retained reveals a lot about the motives behind the murders. They were not frantic and spontaneous but aimed at spreading fear. The presence of the pipe man witnessed by Israel Schwartz at Elizabeth's murder scene may explain this "conspiracy". Once again, the local lingo overheard and reported by Schwartz, reinforces the theory that this was an inside job, not an immigrant's.

The fact that the author of those two Ripper letters also followed the News closely suggests they were literate enough to read, and there goes the local myth of the Ripper being an adult immigrant…

I maintain that the author of the letter wanted the press and the police to believe that he or she was working class, a "chip off the old block", as the Saucy Jack postcard's Irish slang and working-class expressions seem to falsely suggest.

The blood ink metaphor used by the author of the letter "I saved some of the proper red stuff in a ginger bottle over the last job(…) Red ink is fit enough" is also interesting in that it suggests they would have used blood from the last murder to write the letter. It's yet another "freakish" theory that pleases the narrative of the loose monster on the prowl, had it been for the fact blood coagulates in ambient conditions.

Indeed, the "Dear Boss" letter metaphor timeline doesn't fit the chronology of the murders. But more importantly, the reference to the "ginger beer bottle" is quite remarkably anachronistic as it is an unlikely container for an inkpot, and certainly impracticable for dipping a Victorian pen. The author could have poured blood from the same bottle but it would have necessitated a complex freezing, then warming up process to make the blood fluid… This detail might seem insignificant, but if the imagery is correct, the reference to the popular summer drink suggests that the author would have kept the bottle filled with blood since August, when the last murders were committed. Ginger beer was certainly fashionable in summer but wasn't a winter's drink or a psychopath's first choice of spirit. Besides, it is quite unlikely that the bottle filled with blood would have gone unnoticed in lower class communal lodgings without attracting the attention of other tenants or the landlord, and so, even if the bottle had been hidden, due to the pungent smell of rotten blood; the likelihood of ginger beer being an underworld favourite remains faint…

The Legend of Faust comes to mind… Even in the playwright Marlowe's English 1588 adaptation, the gory metaphor seems to point to an educated, financially independent suspect who lived on their own and not in communal lodgings.

The MO

The assumption that the Ripper might have had good knife skills is mainly based on Dr George Bagster Phillips's expert testimony at Annie Chapman's inquest. Conversely, the other murders suggest an indiscriminate evisceration and butchering, as exemplified in Catherine Eddowes and Mary Kelly's violent lacerations to the face.

The popular theory is that the killer must have had some knowledge of anatomy to remove a kidney from the front, as in the case of Eddowes.

In the case of Mary Jane Kelly, however, remains of the stomach were found, which suggests that, even by the medical standards of the period, the Ripper didn't necessarily know what he or she was doing and sharpened his morbid skills "on the job".

Most of the victims are rendered unconscious by a swift cut to the neck. In the case of Annie Chapman, killed at close quarters near the busy Spitalfields market, the victim's face and tongue revealed signs of suffocation. In fact, all victims were never heard crying for help and gagged to prevent screaming.

In his inquest testimony, Dr George Bagster Phillips declares that "there was no evidence of a struggle". For that matter, none of the murder scenes showed such signs. The same doctor aptly comments on the killer's swift blade skills, only to admit later in his testimony that even a surgeon could not have performed such a pelvic organ extraction under an hour, let alone, half an hour, which is the time taken by the Ripper, according to visual witnesses.

This indicates that the killer's main skill is neck cutting and his extraordinary skills were largely that of a skilled assassin who got bolder and sloppier.

The Ripper had no interest for the brass rings stolen from Annie Chapman's dead fingers. Had these had any value, Annie Chapman, whose internal organs showed signs of serious undernourishment, would probably have sold them to eat. The Ripper had a job but enough "spare time" to work at the weekends when he could assassinate prostitutes, with enough warfare skills or insiders' knowledge to avoid police patrols. How he subdued his victims remains speculation, but his M.O. points towards a seasoned assassin who was neither a wanted criminal nor a fearsome predator.

Before the "canonical five" murders, so-called because they show the same MO, the prima facie evidence in the case of Martha Tabram, stabbed 39 times, points to an indiscriminate killing performed with a knife or a dagger. The MO seems to evolve from shell shock stabbing, reminiscent of close contact warfare, to evisceration. The promiscuity of White Chapel could have enabled an indiscriminate shell shock soldier to mutate into a serial killer, intent on assuaging his war symptoms. It might have been something the overweight prostitute said or did to her inebriated punter that prompted the frenzied attack. From then, the motive behind the murders points to gratification in avoiding capture with an escalation in cruelty and pleasure. Evisceration is not present in Martha Tabram's case and therefore doesn't fall under the same M.O. However, the August, 6th murder may have inspired the conspiracy.

Testimonies

In her testimony, Elizabeth Long's describes a forty-year-old man in shabby-genteel clothing and wearing a felt hat. Her impression of the suspected Ripper's clothing suggests second-hand recycled clothes as sold by Jewish traders, much like the once-loved clothing found in charity shops nowadays, which again points to a local.

When forty-seven-year-old Annie Chapman was seen by Elizabeth Long talking to a man in Hanbury Street, the latter describes seeing a man from behind saying 'Will you?' and Anna Chapman's candid face as she was answering 'yes'.

Whatever the exchange was all about, Anna Chapman didn't initially fear for her life. In the case of Elizabeth Stride, William Marshall, a labourer, describes a soft-spoken man wearing a short dark coat and a sailor's hat who was seen talking to the victim an hour before the discovery of her body. She didn't mention any accent.

Police-Constable William Smith describes seeing Elizabeth Stride walking with a man dressed in dark clothes and a deerstalker's hat. Both note that he was of respectable appearance. The most valuable and bone-chilling testimony remains that of Israel Schwartz.

On his midnight walk to work, Israel Schtwartz' testimony intimates that the Ripper could have had an accomplice. He describes two men on the scene of Elizabeth Stride's murder. He is the only one to have actually witnessed a woman being overpowered.

Motive

Most of the murders happened in and around Spitalfields, and especially Wentworth and the back alleys of White Chapel where the "unfortunates" flocked to find money to pay rent for their lodgings.

In the "Dear Boss" letter, the killer allegedly wanted to right a wrong and steer the investigation away from the "leather apron" rumours. Indeed, given the killer's swift knife skills, the leather apron found on the Mary Nichols' murder site could have pointed towards a skilled tradesman which the author of the letter brands as a "joke". But it can be argued that far from steering the investigation away from a local perpetrator, it actually intensifies the theory behind it. What it managed to do is create the legend that the ripper could not be a common man but a scary monster or a lunatic, if one is to believe the Aaron Kosminski theory.

The author of the "Dear Boss" letter uses the word "work" repeatedly. The compulsive serial killer theory fails to reconcile the snarky working-class overtones of the letter and the deferential handwriting. The proposition that the Ripper was an assassin and didn't act alone but on orders seems therefore plausible.

Following a credible confrontation between the all-important witness, Israel Schwartz, the Ripper and another clay-pipe-smoking bystander, a famous graffito was left on the wall to incriminate the Jews, minutes after Elizabeth Stride's murder.

Profile

While the modern profilers suggest a troubled lust killer with mother-figure issues, the killer doesn't have sex with his victims. Assuming that he is the confident cocky and facetiously extrovert author of the letters, it is unlikely that the comings and goings of a mutilated or an impotent man presenting an extreme violent repulsion towards women would have gone unnoticed among the prostitutes, let alone communal lodgings where the "unfortunates" such as Annie Chapman, were alerted to the Ripper's prowling and would have been awake at odd hours of the night.

The MO also indicates that the Ripper knew White Chapel like the back of his hand and could find his way in the squalid area's nooks and crannies well enough to evade the heavy police presence, the vigilante groups, and all despite the acute awareness of the population as to the on-going investigations, which profuse police and newspaper correspondence and articles confirm.

An ex-military mercenary employed by a third party fits the profile. Spitalfields was no place for a doctor or a surgeon, as the area mainly harboured slums and payday lodgings. Therefore, the murderer could have been a resident of the periphery of White Chapel with a good prior knowledge of the area around Spitalfields Market.

The Ripper only killed in the early hours of the morning and on weekends, suggesting regular employment. Annie Chapman who didn't yell at the sight of the Ripper's six to eight inches long knife but instead was pushed against a fence, was probably gagged. Therefore, it follows that the Ripper could approach prostitutes without raising suspicion whether as to his character, accent or appearance, which close-encounter witnesses confirm as "respectable" or at worst "shabby-genteel".

Testimonies about the suspects' voice converge towards a soft-spoken 30 to 35-year-old man. The violence exerted on the victims may just reveal an underlying revenge streak while the overall intent remains "expeditive", which is corroborated in the "Dear Boss" letter where the word "work" is used repeatedly, while the lacerations on Eddowes and Kelly's faces may just be a delaying tactic to prevent identification.

Conclusion

In Dr Robert Anderson's book entitled "The lighter side of my official life" published in 1910, the assistant commissioner of police and chief of the criminal investigation department, who had placed his long-time friend, Donald Swanson, in charge of the White Chapel murders, mentions an important witness: Israel Schwartz.

Israel Schwartz saw the attack on Elizabeth Stride fifteen minutes before the time of death. His testimony is consistent with other testimonies in the case.

Before Israel ran to safety, the attacker called out 'Lipski', a moniker used in those days to taunt Jews. 'Lipski' had become a common anti-Semitic slur since the Polish-Jewish murderer Israel Lipski's hanging a year before.

As the inquests piled up, the canonical five murders seemed to have been expedited. But in his report to the Home Office, on 19th of October 1888, Swanson reports the testimony of Israel Schwartz in full. At 12:45 am, Schwartz saw two men, not one. One man pushed Elizabeth Stride down to the floor while another man, possibly a vigil, lit his clay pipe across the road. The Ripper is said to have called out to the other man on the other side of the road so as to warn him of the unwanted witness Israel Schwartz's presence.

The same pipe man followed Schwartz who ran as far as the railway arch but didn't catch up with him.

The discrepancy between the Chief of the CID and Swanson's account is editorial. By the 1890s, the Ripper's "sanitisation" of White Chapel had prompted more vigilance and safety patrols, sometimes raids, but little controls or checks.

Based on the evidence and investigative elements provided above, my conclusion is that the killer could have been an ex-military mercenary or a member of a gang recruited in a conspiracy to devaluate and cleanse the area around Spitalfields of its unwanted settlers, which would explain the active presence of the pipe man and the assassin at the crime scene of Elizabeth Stride's murder and the relative "laissez-faire" of the police. The overall aim would have been to depreciate the value of White Chapel's properties in a concerted land-grab operation orchestrated by the local mafia involved in the financial deal underpinning the market's expansion.

The Fall

It had been five years since I had first met with Sir Tony Irving, the chief of the Metropolitan Police in person. At the annual charity ball, last Saturday, I caught a glimpse of his tall slender silhouette, arching over his interlocutor, who was much shorter. He was wearing a dapper blue tuxedo and a white bow tie.

I slowly walked up to the socialite who stood like a fly on the wall, holding a glass of champagne in one corner of the chandelier-lit room. There he stood, amidst the sickening baroque Edwardian architectural extravaganza, his back against a faux-porphyry column.

I beat him to the punch with an incisive remark before he could process my name in the Midlands Hotel:

'Not wearing your mess dress tonight, commissioner?'

'I beg your pardon?' he blurted out, as the back of his chaperon vanished into a throng of erect penguins. We had just been introduced by the newly elected mayor; a wet-behind-the-ear maverick who had been parachuted by Westminster.

'Well, get your facts right, young man,' said the grey-haired patriarch, 'there aren't any commissioners any more… Now, if you don't mind…'

Yet, to his credit, his curt remark had been delivered with a velvet glove and impish smile only seasoned socialites can assume. Sir Tony had taken my diatribe in his stride with remarkable sangfroid. He seemed to be musing at his flailing commissioner status in a soirée that felt like a contemporary ballet of overweight ballerinas. Suddenly, my eyes were drawn to some ogees framing a mermaid-like sculpture above the ballroom door. The thought of thousand mermaid hands sowing their magic into the seams of the Mancunian law enforcement glitterati started spinning in my head; although, it could have been the champagne…

As he was lip-syncing echoes of birds' names, leaning on the faux-porphyry column to move away from me, I recalled my first encounter with the prelate…

It happened during the Kinder Scout cases. I was new to public justice and my cassock had yet to be taken off the peg from some mothballed warehouse. Sir Tony had derided my otherworldly talents when I came to see him on the recommendation of Andrew, a DSI who later became part of my congregation.

I moved closer to Sir Tony… Jaws deliberately dropped in irritation at my insistent indiscretion, his carved graphene face turned towards the rostrum as he suddenly snatched a glass of bubbly from a wandering tray, saluting a triad of females who were now standing by the column, eating marble cake:

'Did you know champagne is an excellent anti-oxidant?'

'No, I did not know that, Tony, you son of a bitch…' I muttered between my teeth.

He probably had blotted out all knowledge of my story, not unlike the murdered one he had married, and truth-bubbles somehow took their time to slowly pop up in his mind:

'Actually, I might need your services…' he said unapologetically.

'So what are your plans now you are retired? I mean, are you really retired?' I ventured in the way of conciliatory absolution…

'The grey hair pretty much tells the story… Of course… I… well, there's a whole bucket list of items I have always delayed… One of which is writing my memoirs…'

'Some unsolved cases, maybe?' I said, royally magnanimous.

'Well, now you mention it, hence my asking your business card. But I can't tell you any more at present…'

Although it did cross my mind Sir Tony's mood reversal might have been motivated by an ulterior motive, I was glad to have found my way into his pocket after all…

So it came to pass that I was eventually able to carry on my investigation into Helena's case, not so much because Mike Crompton was impressed with my report, as he had meant it as a prank to ridicule my psychic talents, but it had highlighted the failings of the emerging British detective force who were unable to penetrate the dark matter of these mysterious Victorian crimes or had been told to turn a blind eye…

Crime stories are popular because they open a gash in time… They blur the frontiers between life and death… They interject the newsreader and compose a threatening world at bay, from which no one is safe. They flatter the predator within us as viciously as the prey. They tickle our survival instincts. They repulse us, corroborating our fears of mortality…

Nowadays, sin is no more a crime, yet, in a not such a distant past, committing a sin was a public offense and frowned upon as such. My job as a psychic is to understand how those time fractures come to be. I intervene when human-led investigative processes fail…

Whitsun Sermon

The day following my meeting with the staid Mancunian ex-commissioner, I had got lost in Whaley Bridge. The British countryside was under a thick layer of snow and as usual, British society was unprepared. Some of my favourite shops were closed…

I had gone to the supermarket to buy some wine and vegetables. I had neglected the vegetarian "me" recently, and had to make amends… But, as I tried to reach Glossop and the market, I took the wrong turn, and came face to face with the well-known High Peak British Turkey Butcher of the Year 2006. Once again, the Holy Spirit had intervened: on Market Street, under the thick blanket of snow that had mothballed the whole country, I found a master butcher. It wasn't my usual, but it would do.

And what did I buy instead of the pride of this godsend of a specialist turkey butcher's? Lamb.

I had no excuse. Today wasn't my day. I wasn't thinking straight.

There was more to it than just forgetting to take a turn. I had been living in this area for seventeen years and I still managed to get lost on a regular route. Before I knew it, a strange monologue occupied my out-of-gear mind… I initially put it down on Lent and a fastuous impulse to leave penance behind, but it was my unfinished Whitsun sermon that had led me astray on these roads I knew so well…

Working on the same Whitsun sermon a few hours later, edging impatiently towards despair on my used brown leather executive *Bergère*, glancing alternatively at the coruscating shimmer of light playing on my study's west-facing windows and my computer screen, a strong need for taking stock of my life arrested my sermon in its pastoral tracks…

Was this God's grace or a figment of my imagination that I saw glowing behind the fading glass of my study? I couldn't help being mesmerised by it. I felt God's grace was at hand's reach and yet, it felt too easy…

I suppose I could now look back tenderly at my early days as a psychic and how it all followed its course… Yet, I now had to contend with another hard fact: age. I was knocking on sixty.

Such is life, as the French say, that I couldn't remember what I had done a few hours earlier. If I had been asked what I had for dinner on the spot, I probably would have had to think hard or looked down at my shirt…

However, my first night out in Manchester, some forty years ago, long before I became a vicar, was still fresh in my memory…

I had come from my native Transylvania, where they famously carry garlic garlands around their neck, drink blood and eat slugs. I had gone out for a drink in what I discovered later was the gay district and returned the next day as I felt intrigued…

Retracing my steps, the next morning, in the maze of the foreign city, as newcomers do, irresistibly drawn to the same place, my vagrant mind led me to a spot I had walked past the night before… It was now a deserted crime scene. My fate was sealed when I saw white chalk marks on the floor. Once again, crime had caught up with me. Someone had been murdered the night before…

How I became a psychic investigator with the Manchester metropolitan police is due to Andrew, a DCI whom I befriended soon after I took up the Chapter in this little town of the Peak District…

My first case was a secret consultancy project. No one was supposed to know about it. Everything would be handled in total confidentiality, assured Andrew, a bibulous middle-aged trencherman with a flimsy blond ruffle reminiscent of a monk's tuft, and whose gothic logorrhoea often got him into trouble with his hierarchy. He became my acolyte and a useful vade mecum from then on…

It goes without saying that doubling my vicarious life with a supernatural stipend would prove a balancing act, but my obscure ministry suited well my inquisitive mind…

Generally, if the Met tolerated that I published my psychic tales under a pen name, some officers within the police hierarchy frowned upon publicity… Sir Tony Irving had had sound reasons to refuse seeing me while I investigated the Kinder Scout cases. Yet, I can recall dozens of crimes that would never have been solved without my help.

Embittered by the cynical zeal of my publishers, tied like Sisyphus to the press due to their reckless sensationalism, the then commissioner had disregarded my findings… He had refused seeing me. When MacCloskey finally became a household name, once I had naturalised to become a British citizen, I had to admit the damp English weather had taken its toll. I wasn't the man I used to be, especially since I changed my name and took a famous trade unionist's patronym to better blend in…

Memory lane took me to the verge of dawn… I had somehow managed not to sleep, and I couldn't diffuse an uncanny feeling that Sir Tony would contact me the very same night…

I heard the shearing cry of an owl and decided to check if Sir Tony had sent me an email.

Now, why didn't I check before? It had been sent a few minutes after my departure from the Midland Hotel! Of course, being a psychic, I knew instantly what it contained. I could feel it bubbling under the tip of my mouse. The hardest choice was whether to open it or not…

A psychic draws substance from the psyche, which is defined in psychological terms as both the conscious and the unconscious mind. Any psychic will tell you that the unconscious is a loose term that fails to cover the unchartered territories of the human soul. The term "unconscious" doesn't mean a lot. It is used to cover whatever content the conscious mind doesn't recognise as useful.

Etymology is to blame… The Greek term "psyche" covers everything from thoughts, mind and soul to the unconscious. I have yet to find a scientific definition for my gifts, but experience showed me time and time again that the psyche is a rich cornucopia of knowledge.

Take ichnology for instance. It is the knowledge of trace, much like the scent dogs follow. I am not saying that I can tell what a person has been thinking just by smelling their ass. The last time I explained this to Andrew at the Dog and Partridge, he laughed in my face, making the same stupid joke.

One could argue that I knew Sir Tony was requesting my help to solve the murder of his wife because I had read about it in the press five years before… The commissioner's wife had been found decapitated in the Yorkshire Dales and he had been the prime suspect from the word go. I delayed opening it because I feared his ultimate purpose was to request my services as a man of God and not a psychic. This eventuality frightened me. Why appeal to me now? What was he looking for? Absolution? It didn't make much sense. And yet, if Sir Tony's ultimate purpose was to seek absolution for the murder of his wife, I could be in it for a confessional treat…

Rain

Let's take the elephant in the room: rain… What is rain made of? Rain is to England like sun is to… Oh, bugger it… There's really no need to go there… I am not really keen on explaining why I landed here in this damp cesspit of faux liberalism. Except that this little country is famous for its ghosts… And it might just be down to the abundance of water…

Let me explain… Ions are heavy, sticky molecules… Their interaction creates stronger and more resistant bonds than water molecules. As electro-magnetic fields bend or break hydrogen bonds, dipolar water flows. Ninety-nine percent of our body molecules are water. There is exchange between the outside world and water in our own body, and it alters the way we perceive or feel depending on the magnetic field we find ourselves in. Once you have grasped the premise that water is not such a distant world, it becomes easier to see how spirits form and go. Yes, it is all about perception…

If spirits of dead loved ones and friends exist in this world in any shape or form outside memory, there has to be a scientific explanation that a vicar like myself can live up to. After all, the complex electro-magnetic reaction that modifies our perception of the world around us is the secret of my trade.

I started forming a scientific theory that would withstand any inquisition a long time ago but had yet to find scientific proof. It could be said that our senses are only limited to our own understanding of our intimate chemistry.

While I pondered the need to call back Genesis and the Garden of Eden for my Whitsun sermon, I passed a tentative finger on the mouse. It had come against all odds, despite my social blunder the previous Saturday (I patted myself on the back: always be frank, no matter who you are dealing with). The email remained unopened on my computer, yet I knew it was a desperate move on the part of Sir Tony whatever his facetious façade might have indicated.

As I struggled to keep my mind focused on my writing, the pitter-patter turned into an antediluvian symphony that battered my gutters…

The first time I had to deal with a dead spirit was when my mother died. I knew she had been assassinated by my disjointed stepdad who poisoned her. She was a very religious Roman Catholic. She had always had a thing for priests, and that angered my father who was a communist. I only found out she had been killed many years after her death and I was guided to that revelation, one evening, as I was relaxing after a long day studying for my PhD in religious studies… A voice without sound had talked to me. It felt more like a breeze that touched my soul. I was particularly overwhelmed with confusion, as if, through some strange sudden compulsion, I was forced to connect to a timeless database by an unknown faceless device. It could only be the voice of the Holy Spirit, God's agent, who had decided that I was now old enough to understand…

Since my stepdad was still alive, I visited him to tell him I knew. I looked him in the eye and confronted him. That was the trigger… I was incapable of hating the murderer he really was. It was a turning point…

Of course, I felt angry at first that I should have been oblivious to the real circumstances of my mother's death, but the news had come from somewhere I had never heard of before and this place didn't warrant revenge or hatred…

A few weeks after I confronted my stepfather and our eyes crossed for the last time, he died suddenly. He knew. He knew that I knew and had to die. I left the country never to be seen again. I had found forgiveness in the most unexpected place but still couldn't face the past…

The gift of God led me to a place, and then another, and one thing leading to another, I became a man. It is no surprise I became a vicar. I always wanted to please her. I decided to devote my life to crime solving and the peace of mind of those who are left behind and suffer silently. My account of this part of my life still lies on a dusty shelf, somewhere in the graveyard of publishing failures, in the Amazon Forest of lost dreams…

Andrew should be given credit for the psychic investigation which I published last year, and which Irving must have read. My account of the Kinder Scout cases: a series of disappearances and Victorian-clothed bodies found at the top of the Peak District Mountain, in 2016. Andrew Cunningham, DSI at the Greater Manchester Police Headquarters, on Boyer Street, had called for help and I obliged…

Nothing happens without a reason in heaven. But ultimately, it's Andrew who showed me the ropes of crime detection and investigation.

'As the name suggests,' argued Andrew, who had climbed the ranks of the Northwestern police force to become detective superintendent, 'to be a detective is to detect.'

How I became a part of the world of crime detection is all down to him. We would ramble together on weekends, whatever the weather. We became friends nearly as soon as he became one of my church members.

I can still see it… One Sunday, he walked in through the church doors, followed by a shadow of crime and horror. His purification became a matter of urgency. I could see he was a mess inside when he walked in and distractedly took the July notices from my hands, accompanied by his wife and child. We prayed, we talked, we ate, and little by little, I knew more about his cases than anyone else. The rest is the history of our friendship…

I felt a bit guilty that he should have been demoted because of me, although I came to discover my literary indiscretion was only part of the reason…

I tried hard to anchor my thoughts to the case at hand, despite my hangover and the terrorist attack in Manchester which had killed many young people in the evening. I had to revisit my outlook on the whole sermon…

It had seemed natural to ignore Sir Tony's email, as my suspicions had led me to believe that either he needed a confessor, or he was leading me down the path, but I needed the extra income…

I had perceived self-pity in Sir Tony's voice, and his email confirmed my fears. He required my presence at his mansion.

I quickly called Andrew who had worked on the case in his capacity as a detached CD for Greater Manchester police. We had had a brief chat during the annual ball, and he promised to brief me on the case, should Sir Tony contact me. But he could only tell me what the public and the press already knew. The rest was off limits, even to his friend… I called Sir Tony's number to arrange a visit as soon as I finished reading his email and grabbed a salmon sandwich. I had formed my opinion on his state of mind, and I wanted confirmation that the subject of our meeting together was his murdered wife. I arranged to meet the man who once turned me down…

I had a "Rebecca" moment as I walked up the "gravel gone" driveway leading to Sir Tony's gabled front door. His large heirloom of a cottage didn't feel any less illustrious than Daphne du Maurier's proleptic mind space.

As a diplomatic bribe to make me feel welcome, Sir Tony showed me straight into his solid pine kitchen. But before I had a chance to take a peep at his majestic interior, he wielded a knife under my nose, staring at me with a wild look in his eyes, no doubt, as an extension of secular courtesy between aristocrat and commoners.

'McCluskey! Poached monkfish in goat's milk, no less!' he exclaimed over the cooking pot responsible for the steam on the Georgian windows of his country-cottage kitchen.

'Are you all right?' I asked, alerted by his dishevelled looks.

'I read recently that you had helped a fellow veteran,' he said, eyes riveted on his butcher's countertop.

I watched his hands cutting shallots… He referred to my investigation of the Kinder Scout cases and the case of Private

Jones… I was surprised when he mentioned my attempt at marketing my skills a few years before…

'It wasn't so much an investigation as a peregrination…' I said.

'Are you surprised that I read your book?' he asked, switching on a Breville kettle.

'I have looked you up! What do you think? That I have lost it, is that what you're thinking?'

Sir Tony was now officially retired… In the bare space of his interior, however, he looked undone, wearing in a pair of shabby corduroy trousers and an overstretched mite-gnawed mohair jumper. His tousled hair and excited voice signalled he was on the edge.

'You mentioned an urgent assignment… requiring the services of a professional?' I said cursively, as I met his haggard eyes again.

'Oh, my email, right, if you would like to sit down…' He looked in the direction of a reception room.

I heard him fumbling for mugs in his cupboards as I let myself sink into a large fabric sofa.

'It's the cat that's the problem… Have a sit, McCluskey, sugar?'

'Two, please!'

I was now sitting in a large brown leather sofa beside a green lamp, cup of tea in hand, grandfather's clock bemused. The large Georgian windows overlooking the Sett Valley diffused a misty milky light…

'Would you rather I served you a lemonade, I have some in the fridge, a refreshing Fentiman's, maybe?'

'Oh, no, thank you.'

'It's hot for this time of year, isn't it?'

'Very, even this early in the morning. The cat, you said?'

'Right! The cat! McCluskey, as crazy at it seems, I hear voices when the cat is around. I have visions. My dead wife speaks to me when the fleabag is around. I can't tell you how he came to be part of the family that one, but there you go.'

'My name is actually MacCloskey, sir…' I spelt my name for him.

'Oh, I see… Scottish descent, is that correct? But your accent.'

'Yes, sir, for my sins, I was born in France…'

I took up the name MacCloskey when I naturalised. He must have known that… Although, I was pretty sure that he didn't go as far as to dig out my birth certificate. If he had, he would have discovered that there was more to it than meets the eye…

'How interesting…' he said, retrospectively dubitative about his private feline joke…

Before long, we started talking about the nuts and bolts: the murder of his wife…

'They found her decapitated body in the Yorkshire dales, eighty miles away from my estate.'

'And a terrible time, it must have been…' I said, clearing my throat.

Sir Tony sighed as I looked at a framed enlargement of his wife, an alabaster Asian woman whose face radiated the natural light of a trouble-free soul. As I noticed the picture was on the floor rather than on its usual nail on the wall, he jumped again to his feet…

'Let me get you some Fentiman's! I know it's one of your favourites.'

Of course, Sir Tony's wife, Helena, had no business in Yorkshire, but at the time, the police suspected a lover's tiff or some subsequent wayward blackmail motive behind her brutal death. Had her lover dumped her? Was he targeting her wealth? It was a cold case, and although Sir Tony was police commissioner at the time, his efforts to find the murderer were evidently fruitless.

'Some see in those estranged pets a guider of souls to the afterlife.' I projected tentatively beyond the doorframe to deflect a protracted pussyfooting on the subject of his relived grief. The cat could have become a psych pomp, a psychic vehicle for Sir Tony's late wife. I had heard of cases where grieving people attributed strange spiritual qualities to pets who shared their life. As for those voices, they probably came from his head. But I didn't say that verbatim…

'What if they were the voices of the dead calling?' he said.

'Sir Tony, you have been living on your own for a while now, haven't you?' I asked him as soon as he returned from his kitchen with lemonade.

'As you know, I have been consistent in looking for the murderer of my wife, but… Life has been an underground chary of shit and shower gel since her passing away. I have not had time for police work.'

'Those voices are your subconscious calling for spirituality, sir. Hearing voices means you crave for a link back to the soul. In essence, it is a safety mechanism of the subconscious. Is it quite true that her presence in the Yorkshire Dales was unexplained, wasn't it? It may be that you are looking for some closure and that you associate your cat with her… Well, let's say, it has become a go-between…

Animals can't talk, so their silence feed our imagination. For all we know, it could remind you of her…'

'Pussy?' said Sir Tony, abruptly.

'I meant comforting presence, sir… I have read the report and the files on the case. I have a very good friend in the ranks. Are there any new elements I am not aware of?'

Sir Tony kept silent, no doubt clinging to the orient of his pain like a precious compass, judging by the look of self-pity in his eyes. After all, he had been the prime suspect in the case. As my frankness had already paid off, I ventured a bold statement:

'You feel guilty, don't you?'

'Guilty?' he said as the blood rushed to his forehead, seemingly alive for the first time since I arrived.

'I felt magnanimous! Letting her go on a weekend with her lover is quite princely, wouldn't you say?'

'I suppose so…'

'Here's my guilt, MacCloskey: although, I am conscious that she might have felt guilt herself, part of the reason why I followed her that night was to put things right in her heart. Nothing more… And I failed!'

'I understand,' I said with genuine empathy.

'Now, what is the way forward?' he asked. 'I don't want these voices anymore. I can't take it!'

Prevaricating as little as possible, I explained that, for the avoidance of doubt, I wasn't a shrink but a psychic, and that we would have to use hypnosis to recollect the events preceding his wife's death to unofficially exonerate him before anything else. I didn't use those words exactly, but I did insist my prescription would involve revisiting the events to make sense of the very last hours she lived. I meant to probe

Sir Tony's elaborate tale of innocence, of course, but if I had to play the devil's advocate, it would be on my own terms.

'Does that involve a truth serum, MacCloskey?' he joked.

'How else?' I said undeterred. 'We have to start somewhere…'

'Seriously, what does it involve exactly?'

I had expected that question, so instead I pitched my extra-sensory perception. I expected him to say something in the line of 'How about you cut the crap, hey?' or 'How about you use your so-called psychic powers to find her head?'

I delicately put down my cup of tea in its saucer. I was never a staunch tea drinker, and coffee made my prostate swell.

'We will find the murderer. That is exactly what I intend to do with your help. But for that, I need to connect to the knowledge that is out there, in the invisible world of spirits. You knew her best, you loved her, and you can still access an unchartered world that you two shared, somewhere lost in time, eternal time, I mean…'

When I returned home, crime scene reports in hand, I became excited at the idea of a new case. Sir Tony's unconditional love for his unfaithful wife was now evident to me… He made me think of the Saint Bernard who never stops searching for the missing victims of an avalanche, except perhaps, for a juicy truffle in a young bush, which, as the rumour went in the county, was one of his favourite delicacies. We are all sinners…

I meant to talk about love and especially the meaning of the expression "to fall in love", to illustrate my point to my congregation for Sunday's sermon, when I realised Koroshiya and I were the only example I had at hand. I realised at this stage of my sermon that I had forgotten last night's washing in the washing machine and that Koroshiya would probably tell me off for my absentmindedness, when I suddenly remembered she had left several years ago. This is how Sir Tony and I connected so well. We were both mature single men with secrets. Our paths were now intertwined…

'What if Genesis was but an end in itself?' I would argue to my indolent congregation… To imply a reading of the Bible from Revelations backwards amounted to reading from right to left, and before you know it, I would be called a denier who exhorted his disciples to read the sacred book like Japanese people read their papers…

But why do people 'fall' in love, I would exhort my congregation. Why not 'rise' in love, to heavenly realms?

How long will this world live? What if Genesis wasn't the beginning but the end? Sunday's trinity sermon promised to be a decisive do-loop…

I couldn't help thinking about our own Eden, Koroshiya and I… Knowing Eden is all about understanding the nominal difference between cupids and cherubs… Cupids are facetious toddlers with cheeky smiles flanked with chicken wings, cherubim predate the fall while cupids herald love.

But guilt is evil's gilt, and evil is useless… Conversely, good is nothing without evil. Good only made it to the score table by contrast. Yet, one cannot help noticing that evil has a life of its own and that sometimes good can come out of it.

Koroshiya's departure from our Eden made me a man of God. In truth, the original sin is a gift of knowledge from the Creator, albeit a facetious one. There you have it. Cherubim, not cupid, my friends… Everyone mistakes the granted cherub guarding the entrance of the Biblical Garden for an angel of love, but none see it as a warning. It is no cupid. See it smirk at eternity… Cherubim are four-winged angels and sit by the Creator in Heaven. We have fallen. Get over your dirty laundry!

Hypnosis

Now, I had jotted down several titles for this chapter of my diary: “Lying in the name of truth”; “on behalf of my heart”; “A decrepit mind”, all of which have been duly recorded on my high-tech smartphone.

But by the time I resumed my writing, this all seemed perfunctory, especially now that the sun was washing my patio with light.

I was sitting in my office, looking for some red-tape loose ends to tie up. Sir Tony texted me of his imminent arrival from his car. I greeted him outside church and showed him through the aisles and down the basement where I have my office.

Sir Tony was in a sombre mood… We chatted about the weather and the decorations made by the community teams in preparation for Thursday’s feast. He had some business to attend to in the afternoon, so, unsurprisingly, he disregarded his instant coffee and grabbed one of the plastic folding chairs…

‘Are you a Christian, sir?’ I said, point blank.

‘My family was Catholic at some point of our history, yes,’ said Sir Tony, hesitantly.

It made no difference whether he was or not, except that in some circumstances, it could be quite rewarding to convert an atheist. Throw me the first stone if you will but I can't be blamed for wanting to kill two birds with one.

After a prayer, Sir Tony sat deeper in his chair as he began homing in onto his deeper self with my help…

The ex-commissioner entered in a trance-like state almost without a fight. I put it down on his exhaustion and his internal battle with grief and guilt.

'Where were you on the evening your wife died?'

'Down the alley, towards the pub…'

'That was before you talked to your wife… What did you do after you talked to her… in the restaurant?' I stressed the word "after" to give him time to process the meaning of it, as under hypnosis, the mind often wanders off to *la la land* where timelines are blurred.

'I followed her…'

'Where to?'

'To our bedroom.'

'Bedroom, where?'

'She was sprawled on the bed with her legs wide open…'

'Sir, was it after you talked to her at the restaurant? Where were you after the restaurant?' I said, anxious to get back on track.

'At the hotel…'

'Which hotel. Does it have a name?'

'Yes, George…'

'What did you do at the hotel?'

'I came home… No… I… waited in George's lounge with his son…'

'His son, what was his name?'

'Rupert…'

During hypnosis, you cannot rely entirely on words; you must feel the subject's emotions, their twitches, spasms, facial expressions… Words are just empty boxes filled with a substance as malleable as water. They are prone to collocation and transfer of meaning.

"Rupert" might have had another meaning, another acceptation in Sir Tony's language. Just like George. George wasn't a hotel but George's place. I would find out about George's restaurant later, during my investigation…

I learned later from Andrew that "Rupert" was the name of Helena's lover. We both knew George's son was called Jimmy. Rupert might have had some other bearing. For all purpose intended, it could have placed Rupert with Sir Tony at the time of his wife's disappearance. I made a note of it and promised myself I would look at the case files again…

'And then? You left the restaurant? You left George's restaurant. What then?'

'I came home…'

'Directly?'

By this time, truth was huffing and puffing behind Sir Tony's forehead…

'No, I stopped.'

'Where?'

'Near a field… It was late… It stank…'

'What stank?'

'No… The field stank! I must puke.'

'OK. Then what happens next?'

'I am driving towards the house… It's blurred, the road… I… I drive slowly… A kerb… My house… Going to bed…'

'You drive back and go to bed, that's it?'

'No, I have a glass of milk.'

Sir Tony had now become pale and was drained out of his life force and so was I. Since he showed signs of extreme exhaustion, I had no other choice but to stop there and bring him back to safety. He opened his eyes and looked around. He thanked me and asked if he had done all right and left without so much as a goodbye, as if nothing mattered. It wasn't conclusive by any stretch of the imagination. In fact, the session had been resoundingly disappointing by any standard. But it was a first step… At least, my mind was appeased as to his character. He had a glass of milk! He probably didn't, his mind was hanging by a thread to its identity, confused about his sense of self, clinging to some comforting distant childhood memories…

I prayed on the wet tarmac, waving, and searching for what seemed an eternity for clues, nose in the wind, or for the certainty that he was innocent as I waved goodbye…

Given the result, I had no choice but to revisit the details of the case with a new approach, down to a tea. Had he admitted to killing his wife, the case would have been straightforward… On the other hand, there was a high probability that I could be dealing with a calculated murderer whose subconscious had blotted out the whole incident. This prospect was certainly blood chilling… There can be no sorcerer's apprentice in this line of trade. I am a vicar, a man of God. I stand at the gates…

Needs must, the very same afternoon, I contacted Mike Crompton, the DSI in charge, on a need-to-know basis, to tell him I had my doubts about Sir Tony's innocence, and he thanked me for it. I never act outside the law… I then left a message on Sir Tony's answering machine to arrange my stay at his mansion the next weekend, so I would be granted unfettered access to his troubled mind.

When he asked me to postpone, I arranged for another psychic session after my holidays.

I was elated despite my tiring session with Sir Tony. Not so much because of my results, which were poor, but because I had not performed hypnosis for a long time. I started cooking to wind down. As sure as the Euphrates and the Tigris rivers meet downstream, I realised I had marinated the lamb in a teriyaki and jerk chicken marinade. Japanese condiments meet Jamaican spices – I must have been at sixes and sevens and that showed in my cooking!

I had missed a trick, nevertheless… Looking at the case files in my lounge, after dinner, which somehow made the whole affair even more toxic, since I never took any work outside of my study, apart from my cherished King James' version, I soon found myself pouring wine from my favourite decanter with the Bacchus head spout…

The name of Sir John Irving's late wife's lover was Rupert Sutherland.

Rupert turned out to be a wealthy Manchester estate agent, known among the police for his relentless evacuation orders in the dilapidated buildings of Manchester city.

Looking for information on Rupert's social media pages, I found an interesting unrelated link to a freedom of information request sent by a disgruntled taxpayer to the council, and following the link to their correspondence, I fell upon Rupert's complaint regarding the publication of a list of 9604 long-term empty buildings in the Manchester area. I surmised that the taxpayer in question worked in social care and that Rupert had protested because he had rather sit on his empty properties for tax-relief purposes rather than open them to squatters and homeless people, which got me thinking… Rupert and Sir Tony might have known each other…

I also found out that Rupert had shamelessly displayed compromising photos of Helena on his Facebook pages, all duly noted by the police in their case files.

According to the same files, Rupert hadn't been a prime suspect because he had not left his room above George's gastro pub on the night of the murder. George was adamant… It seemed in this case that all pivotal testimonies hinged around the publican's timeline but George had refused to see me… No matter how hard I tried – I even visited his pub with Andrew – he had nothing more to say.

Incidentally, one evening, Andrew and I decided to talk to his son, Jimmy. Jimmy had chaperoned his father's cousin while he sobered up, after his confrontation with his wife. Jimmy could be found at a motorbike garage, according to his girlfriend, Sally, the sassy generously bosomed happy-go-lucky chick who directed us. Andrew had already talked to him during his investigation, but he agreed that George's testimony had as many holes as a Swiss cheese, enough to warrant another chat…

By the time we reached the top of the hill, up the Bolton countryside lane, heavy smoker Andrew was puffing smoke out of his ears.

'What's the matter, Andrew? Are you out of steam, already?'

'You wanted to park downhill … You know Mike is breathing down my neck, right?'

'Why is that, Andrew?'

Andrew raised his eyebrows and sighed.

‘Since I missed my deadline for filing a report with the commander…’

‘I see… So is he breathing down your neck or blowing smoke up your ass again?’

I realised how stupid my question was since he was accompanying me on a case where he shouldn’t have been in the first place.

‘I am doing this as a favour, and to be honest, this isn’t the best way back into the lap of the Gods.’

‘Good on you, Andrew, way to go… The devil is in the detail; don’t you know that? You can’t miss deadlines. So why don’t you start by quitting the fags, hey?’

I saw an opportunity to spur Andrew’s faith…

‘Come to our power prayer sessions, it will do you good.’

We found Jimmy in greasy overalls at the garage, working on a cut-down. Jimmy saw us and started the engine.

‘Can’t really talk, right now!’ he shouted as we drew nearer the garage.

‘Stop the engine!’ said Andrew, crimson.

‘I can’t, the kill switch is not working!’ Jimmy shouted from his greasy promontory.

After a little squabbling, Andrew took Jimmy away from the noisy bike.

‘What we wanna know is what your father has told you what to say in your statement.’ Said Andrew, in his customary Mancunian lingo.

Jimmy turned pale. His tousled hair and chav demeanour weren’t fooling anyone. He was a daddy’s boy despite his skinny jeans.

‘What did he tell you to say in your testimony five years ago when Sir Tony’s wife died?’

‘Oh, that! Nothing…’ he shrugged.

‘Come on, give over, they are reopening the case. We have testimonies that tell us your father couldn’t possibly have watched over Irving the night of the murder, since he was front of house serving customers,’ I said, squaring him in the eye.

‘That’s right! But I said exactly that to the inspector. I don’t know what my father told you… like… five years ago!’

‘Well now, and five years ago, there was a murder. I was in charge of the investigation,’ said Andrew. ‘I should know!’

‘Well, visibly, you don’t,’ said Jimmy, fumbling for excuses in the pockets of his overalls. But he seemed genuinely disinterested…

‘Can’t you tell us anything about Irving’s state of mind that night?’ I asked.

‘He was all drunk and weird, like he had seen red. We looked after him well, don’t you worry. He didn’t drive back until he was sober. His wife even wanted to drive him home. He was pissed off, that’s all.’

‘You’re saying it’s Helena who drove him back?’

Andrew’s double chin started wobbling with excitement. How could his inspectors have omitted that in their report?

‘She said she would… I’ve got no idea if she did or not.’

‘So, what time did he leave?’ I asked impatient at this deflective attitude.

‘I dunno, he stayed until he was sober, 4:30 maybe. Hey, it’s been five years, see what I’m saying?’

We left Jimmy to his engine. Andrew promised he would get down and dirty with George again. I doubted inspectors had omitted such important information.

I remember Andrew stepping in church at the time and it wasn't pretty. He must have overlooked a few details in his own investigation… He had delegated too much…

I mean, seriously? As a police officer, Sir Tony knew how the time of death would be calculated. Presumably, had Sir Tony been the killer, he would certainly have thought of a more solid alibi. Yet, his only covered part of the window of opportunity in the hours of the morning of September 20th when his wife was killed. This was the conundrum I was left with…

His wife left the hotel at 12:30 pm, half an hour before he finally left the restaurant at 1 am, according to George, the owner. I thought about the timeline on our way back to New Mills…

Sir Tony who would have been indeed charged if the Yorkshire dales were not three hours' drive away.

This could not have exonerated him since the body discovered the next day by a rambler at 10 am, left an estimated eight-hour window to deposit the body minus three hours.

Nothing could be discounted.

Given the shadow of doubt hovering over Sir Tony's whereabouts, he became the prime suspect. The strange fact about that investigation method is that he should have remained so, and not be exonerated.

Then again, he was the commissioner… What I gathered from my second meeting with Sir Tony is that it wasn't George who babysat the cuckold until he sobered up, but his son, Jimmy. It was a busy night and George managed the floor until late, which a few of his friends who stayed in camera after hours confirmed. This was elucidated by Andrew who spoke to the late-night revellers…

When we asked Jimmy's girlfriend the same question, she said that Sir Tony left the restaurant half an hour earlier than recorded on her boyfriend's statement, at 12:30 am.

Jimmy had wrestled with Sir Tony who wanted to take off. He had looked at the time, impatient to meet his girlfriend back at their apartment and called her to ask her to wait for him as it could be a long night. When he called her again, it was 12:30 am.

Yet, George told the police he had spent the rest of the night with him, making sure he didn't drive back. So, either Jimmy got the times wrong, or George lied on purpose, or both. Either way, he told Jimmy what to say and covered for Sir Tony. Why the police didn't pursue this line of enquiry is telltale…

They were covering for Sir Tony… If Sir Tony was indeed innocent, this lapse of judgment on the part of the Greater Manchester's police was damning…. It meant the case could be thrown out.

On the other hand, if he was indeed innocent, his handling of the case as a commissioner might have been perceived as sloppy. Even if he had meant to clear his name…

What's more, another local, an estate agent by the name of Mellor, stayed after closing hour at the pub and confirmed that George minded his guests until 1:50 am and couldn't possibly have been watching over his cousin. I knew Mellor, as he had requested my service on a couple of occasions before. Businessmen sometimes use my gifts before an important investment. It is part of the perks of being a well-acquainted psychic…

What did Sir Tony do after he left the restaurant? Why did George lie to the police?

Although, they didn't find any evidence of a body in his rented car, or on his clothes from the night of the reckoning with his wife, or in his house, a huge question mark as heavy of the sword of Damocles was still hanging over Sir Tony's head…

He could have used another car. He could have left the restaurant at the same time as his wife, follow her and abduct her to commit the crime. But none of that transpired. He had a figment of an alibi and it seemed enough…

The Slavonic dance, op 72 "Dumka" in E minor certainly reverberated the *molto espressivo* mood I was in when I returned to my office that night, after yet another hypnosis with Sir Tony. Needless to say, I dealt with thorny cases in my lifetime but nothing as heart-breaking as a man who can't remember whether he killed the woman he loved or not.

Now I always thought my mission in life as a vicar was to help others go through theirs, indeed, as the saying goes, to carry their cross… And so I have done without so much as a thank you… The great circle of hollowness is the school of life…

But separation feels like a part of you has died. I should know… It is not actually a death but another fall. Adam and Eve must have been pissed off at each other after the Fall. To fall in love… Every time a man falls in love, he falls out of heaven… The prospect of falling that accompanies the sacred expression is what we earthly thrill-seekers crave the most. It's the reeling, the dancing with the hope of vanquishing death, the multiplying and the thriving that civilisations seek. It is all encompassed in a grain of divine inspiration and yet, it is all happening under the evil eye of the four-winged dragonfly cherubs. It hovers over a swamp amidst the bulrush and the cat's tongues.

Where a church service was usually enough to give me the impetuous to write the next Sunday's sermon in the same breath by simply taking the pulse of the faithful crowd at St James, this time, I did not manage to find inspiration for this Corpus Christi revelation. The diary of my psychic investigation of the murder of Sir Tony's wife had taken too much of my time… I could see that now. I revisited my writings of the day that had just dissolved into dawn but couldn't help forming a mental picture of Koroshiya, sluggishly dropping her brown leather boots on the doormat, laid as a time-travel platform over the terracotta tiled floor of our faded Mediterranean chic interior. The stark reality of her ghostly return hit me like a brick. Even the torn sounds of dusk's ribbons whirling and twirling in the dimly lit sienna red interior seemed to carry her voice: "but it will smell mouldy if you don't take them out of the washing machine now!" I could have argued to my fellow Christians that I had been hit for six with Sir Tony's predicament. If I kept that side of my life secret – sometimes even the tightest ship can hit unseen riffs – Sir Tony's case added insult to injury. But that was to be expected, I might say. Still for now, I found him still pretty much alive and kicking during our now weekly hypnosis session…

A few hours after my sermon, a robin visited the church garden. Here, at the fringe of the Peak District, a robin had perched on the bench, near the back door. Before he turned its rusty gorge towards me, I felt its disarray.

I said, 'Hello little robin. Are you looking for your other half? Are you sad?'

◆◆◆

The proof I am getting old beyond my age is that I smeared my trousers hem while urinating this afternoon. I had to change…

Native American Indians' initiation process into adulthood involves a "Night of fear" passage where they lay naked in the wilderness, on their own, for a whole night, whatever the weather, so they may face and overcome their fears of the dangers of nature lurking around. It is symbolic of course, as we have several such ritualistic nights during our lifetime. But let's say that, according to Native American Indians, if you have overcome your fears once, you're a dreadnought.

I remembered this little axiom from Wa'na'nee'che, the Navajo Shaman. When you throw a stone in a deep pond, you will see circles at the surface of the water. These circles are a metaphor for life. You may see several circles radiating from the centre where you have thrown the stone but make no mistake; they are all connected and linked to larger circles that cannot be seen yet…

For life is not just one circle…

I was glad Andrew had entered a new circle in his life. Quitting smoking would certainly help him clear his mind. As for I, I began to face the prospect of becoming old alone. Wa'na'nee'che's point is that you should never get stuck in one endless circle, rather let your mind radiate towards the bigger circles.

I cannot tell how sometimes I deplore those gifts I have. It just strikes when you least expect it. But hollowness is the key to my Christian faith. It is a place where fear must be conquered, as the human soul is an imprint of God. A man of God is an empty shell filled with the light and knowledge of otherness. And this knowledge can only be achieved though hollowness…

After Andrew and I spent the afternoon regurgitating our interview with Jimmy at the Dog and Partridge, while socialising at his home, over a fresh cod dish cooked in home-made tomato sauce (red onions, cherry tomatoes and Teriyaki sauce – I kept the latter ingredient secret from his wife) and buttered wilted spinach, I told them no matter hard I tried to elevate myself to God, a last-ditch attempt from the Divine Comedy genius always seemed to add an eleventh-hour quip to bring me back down to earth.

Andrew and his wife were questioning me quizzically about my love life, and I told them how my own love circles always seemed to bring me back to the original circle and the first throw of the stone, Koroshiya…

Her departure might have happened six years ago, but I was still in love with her, and I wasn't ready yet to trade my love for anything else, except the kind of transcendental love I had for Christ and his mission.

I became aware that a new cycle had just began to radiate when that young couple who had just moved in down the road – there are only three houses on Cross Street – became under attack from a wandering spirit whom I had had dealings with a few years before Koroshiya and I separated.

My new young neighbours were usually communicative, and I suppose, hopeful, and rightfully exhilarated by the birth of their first child, but never as sullen or despondent as they seemed to be that day. That's how I knew something was amiss. This time, I had seen the tension you see only between those who are haunted. I sensed it straight away. I felt a change in their aura so I pricked my ears… Add to their unusual demeanour (I wrote this word all over again three times, as I couldn't remember its spelling), the fact that the birds had not sang this very morning as usual, alarm bells started ringing…

The ghost was that of an old man. I can see it clearly from the inside, as if I were privy to his thoughts, looking from the street, into the window of time. Let me tell you they are not pretty… I am talking about a cantankerous sociopath from a distant age, probably as far as Victorian times. It is a spirit of the vagrant type, if any. Most are attached to a place and return in part or in whole thanks to some magnetic storm.

What he was looking for is not so much of importance as the reason why he was looking for it…

Sir Tony's Adieu

I visited Rhodes and Crete. I found some well-deserved peace on Mount Ilias, in a small chapel named after the great prophet Elijah, on the island of Rhodes. As usual, the Lord guided his servant on his scooter, and he didn't disappoint…

I felt under the aegis of his illustrious name as soon as I walked in under the gilded vault, which in the searing heat, felt like dipping my soul into a cool bath. I could say more about this feeling that comes with entering a cool church in a searing heat, which, to my northern hemisphere constitution, is unusually welcome, as I am more accustomed to entering a warm church on a freezing cold morning.

Greek Orthodox churches are adorned with the beauty of Christ shining in the wilderness. This little chapel in the quiet outback felt like an oasis on the island where Paul cast anchor. Some claim he preached the Gospel inland. Others say that his ship just moored there from Cos, on his way to Jerusalem, on his third missionary journey…

I could talk about my trip on the yacht I skipped for a few miles, thanks to the kindness of the owner who noticed I had the old sea dog in me, but that would be deliberately avoiding the terrible news I learned when I returned from my annual holiday, at the end of June…

Lord Irving had killed himself.

I read of it in the press, and even messaged the journalist who wrote the article. My DSI friend, Andrew, confirmed he had died a few days after my departure.

Even after multiple accounts, I still could not believe it. Sir Tony was no more. I was afflicted, and I suppose I will be for the rest of my life…

It all made sense to me two days after my return from Greece, when I received two diaries which were kept from the investigation until now… They remained untouched on my desk for a few hours at least, thanks to the warden, John. I just couldn't get my head around it. Reading the papers didn't help…

Another piece of exceedingly bad news concerned my friend Tim, the pastor of the Evangelical church down the road, who had been charged with embezzlement. The press portrayed him disrespectfully as a scoundrel who lived it large on the Holy Spirit's account. According to the gutter press, his evangelical church had become the Church of Barabbas.

I was not able to open the diaries just yet, let alone contemplate what their content might hold without feeling sick with vertigo from peering down at the magnitude of what just happened. And who keeps a diary these days, apart from old relics like me and maybe a few teenagers and scrapbook-mad mums?

But Sir Tony's diary was no scrapbook, as for his wife's; it's a miracle that led to the conclusion of this investigation. Imagine little old MacCloskey coming back from holidays to learn of Sir Tony's death in the Newspaper, and two days later, receiving a parcel from the same! Now, don't get me wrong. I have nothing against surprises, but this felt like entertainment gone mad!

I had to settle my glasses on my nose before I feverishly prized open the manila paper package which was about the size of a shoe box and faggoted with cooking strings, my suitcases still unpacked in the lobby…

The box contained two spiral-bound notebooks and a letter. It was all it contained and yet, it was the two lives of a loving couple torn apart by jealousy and I suspect, envy.

As for the letter, it didn't make any sense at first. It was the letterhead of some conveyance firm, which I checked out promptly on my smartphone. The body of text was handwritten. I soon realised that he had meant to lead me to the conclusion that I had been chosen only because it could have been detrimental to his conveyance arrangements or something along those lines, not that I knew yet who his estate would be passed on to, as the whole picture was still a blur…

In any case, it wasn't the admission of guilt I was expecting; this is what it said:

"Inside this box you will find my resolute admission of the truth. I did not do it. But there are elements of this case in which I have a responsibility. If I strongly suspect the case to have been stonewalled and mothballed, it wasn't my doing. The reason why is still unclear to me, but I have strong suspicions that it came from higher up in the hierarchy, and by that, I mean, not so much the police but the government. They will always have their hands clean, no matter what they do, for the simple reason that if one head falls, another grows back. I will spare you the details of my anti-establishmentarianism. Just so you know, I made no bones about your heresy, but I believe you and I are of the same vein.

Just take care of these diaries, as they will not only prove my innocence, but could also lead you to the real culprits. I must warn you that once you have cleared the ground and identified the henchmen and their modus operandi, you will hit a brick wall. I have enough experience as a commissioner to know where the buck stops in the grand scheme of policing. In my diary, you will find some elements of truth as to why some of my fellow countrymen might have wanted my wife dead. I have come to the fatal conclusion that I will never find peace in this world and that my life has reached a dead-end. Let's call it a deadlock. Thank you for your assistance and sorry for deriding you a few years ago when you came on the force as a consultant psychic. I should have seen you for what you were. I had little time for open-mindedness at the time, which, far from excusing my behaviour, may partly explain why I treated you like a peddler. I am happy to see you are a man of God after all, and this is why I confided in you. If you are the man I think you are, and you probably have seen "behind the curtain", to use your expression, so you know already why Ling (the one you know as Helena, was killed…)"

The Mancunian Way

I resented driving to Manchester. But the atmosphere after the terrorist attack was inspiringly defiant.

Imagine a mellifluous Kora playing a theme by Bach; Muslim women dragging gaudy suitcases in their burqas; haggard homeless people whispering in your ear like doomed prophets; and Reverend MacCloskey, simply taking it all in: the industrial heritage, the Neo-Gothic, the Edwardian baroque, the Art Nouveau, and blending in, among the swarms of shoppers and ant-like visitors carrying their cultural identity in and out of shops and art museums, under the watchful eye of history. A prostitute even stopped me in the street to ask me directions to her new parlour job!

I imagine it wasn't any different to a big City like Hong Kong in the 1990s where the connections of Miss Ling alias Helena enabled her to enter the world of Sir Tony's tweed intelligentsia.

They met in the City of Pearl's notorious Repulse Bay hotel in 1993 where they got married. He describes her as a woman who knew what she needed rather than what she wanted. But while I was reading the suicide candidate's last diary entries, my perspective shifted to the life of Helena alias Miss Ling…

Seeing her picture as I paused on the press articles covering their wedding in some glass cathedral of the Pearl of the Orient, I understood that a woman who knows what she needs is not necessarily a maverick. I have some experience of the female genus, and looking at their wedding photo, it doesn't take a genius to see that she was of the same sex as Sir Tony and I.

It was the first time I saw her as a young lady boy, and until I had further evidence from Andrew, I couldn't not call her otherwise.

I guess it was time I realised this case was about her, and not about Sir Tony. The first detail that struck me on the wedding picture was her waist, suspiciously too large for a woman her age and who never had children. Her shoulders, her hands and fingers told the same story, and to my knowledge, she didn't play the piano, nor did I see any at Sir Tony's.

I spent long minutes scrutinising their diaries but they neither mention babies or the possibility thereof. I read both diaries right up to the end to form a complete picture, but even her borrowed swaying gait and constricted smile on this *cliché* taken at the Repulse Bay hotel seemed to tell a different gender story… By the time of the handover of the city to China, Sir Tony and Mrs Irving had returned to London. She called herself Helena by then.

Sir Tony explains how he had her first name changed as part of a prenup contract. However noble Sir Tony's commitment to cherish his wife Helena may have been, there is no doubt he wanted her to disguise her true identity.

It is mirrored in Miss Ling's diary where she described her husband as an attentive companion and a gentleman whose "manners and regards for her would have made her friends jealous had she had any".

She never quite understood the point of changing names, and referred to herself as Ling, her true Hong Kong name, on the title page of her diary.

As for her origins, I learned that her parents were Chinese. They had moved from Shenzhen to Hong Kong in the 1960's when the demand for labour seemed unquenchable and the population growing exponentially.

"Miss Ling" had a good upbringing. In her diary, she told whoever she was writing to about the communist riots, as well the lavish festivals and natural disasters forming the backdrop of her bourgeois education. I can see great improvement in her English throughout the years. She had probably been brought up for such a marriage from an early age.

Despite her being a prostitute at the age of 18 after the death of both her parents in a car accident, she never stopped dreaming she would marry her prince charming. That, I gleaned in Sir Tony's diaries, which I assume were for my privileged eyes only… The police never found those as none of the case files mentioned them.

As I was reading the two diaries side by side for the purpose of my investigation, I could not help shedding a tear with Miss Ling when she recalled the accident and her dissolute lifestyle, and how Sir Tony nurtured her on the road to Damascus. But it took me weeks to go through all this dense and precious material…

◆◆◆

I've tried to find names for the sounds this July rain that my conscience noticed following the diaries: gargle, drip, pattering, but is it not true poetic licence for my soul to shake off its shackles? If I had to describe the rain further, I could use the words "laughter", "giggles", instead of "pelting" and "thrumming", which are inadequate verbs to express the delicate beauty these sounds bring to my heart. It brings tears of joy thinking about my own wedding. It reminds me of her voice. I wish my mother had been around to see her. Your mother is a kind soul… Our love was tainted by this God-forsaken cesspool of hatred against everything that is pure and innocent.

This country is not Jerusalem, my sweetie… The deception is beginning to crack at the seams… There is a wind of fascism and ultra-nationalism blowing through the cracks of the traditional English upholstery.

I believe I accepted this mission because my extra-sensory abilities do not allow me backing out. Remember, when I spoke to you of a calling from God? Well, "us", mere mortals are under the spell of his "agent": The Holy Spirit.

Anything we do against is the real sin. As Eden is carved in our souls, everything else is immaterial. We are subsumed to His word. In Judaism, they call it "Divine inspiration". This is a loose term…

I remember when I was a child that, however little I knew about the world I lived in was enough to make me happy, even if I didn't know anything by men's standards. Did it matter if I knew nothing of the world beyond my reach? You may ask: how is it possible that anyone would want knowledge that is useless? Well, I guess it's about growing up in a society where others need you to better themselves. It is not just about making a living; it's about making a difference.

I believe I was not only chosen by Sir Tony, but by the Holy Spirit, and that whatever evil he committed, there had to be a bigger picture. How wrong was I… I will tell you later of my slow and patient anointment and how I became a vicar, but for now, I must resume with the case at hand… Love, Daddy…

◆◆◆

Sir Tony's case was never an ego-trip on my part, but a descent into a fathomless pit I welcomed as yet another victory in the name of the truth.

As Jesus knew St John the Baptist's fate since Paneas, I had to carry on walking towards her tomb so I could learn more about this man's curse.

Therefore, here I am. But I am profligate with words… I should get to the point.

Sir Tony's wife was decapitated… As much as it pained me to imagine such a beautiful creature without a head, the case had to be dissected methodically. So, the first step was to research criminal annals for similar cases. An empirical study of decapitation would tell me more about the criminal mind behind this execution, as I had no doubt that it was indeed a bona fide punishment where motive and method were intimately connected.

The punishment of beheading and quartering in England historically befell traitors. The English "Bloody code" even included "being in the company of gipsies for one month" an offence punishable by death until the first half of the 18th century. Beheading was abolished in the second half of the 19th century for traitors, or so I learned from Wikipedia.

The last decapitation by axe took place in Derby, in 1817. Derby is south of here, Sir Tony's county. This historical spinning-worm took me to Sir Tony's family tree, but I gave up after a few hours as I am not one for heraldry. It feels like barking up the wrong tree. Indeed, I found no worthy coronet in Sir Tony's ancestry…

It would have been useless knowledge as the victim is his wife, not him. But it was interesting to note how the last decapitation to take place in England in 1817 was that of Jeremiah Brandreth, a Luddite who led a protest march to the tower, in order to overthrow the establishment and end misery for weavers and textile workers.

If the government of the time made a martyr of a movement that had started with industrial sabotage by brandishing his head as a reminder for the masses, Karl Marx would later resurrect the Luddites in Das Kapital, arguing that the machines would someday become man's competitor himself.

A decapitation is no small business. All in the forensic report, which was passed on to me by the same Andrew whom I shared a B&B room with, near Ben Nevis, only last month, seemed to indicate the head had been severed post-mortem. Therefore, the possibility of an accident had to be discounted.

Sir Tony was no Luddite, of course, let alone a machine-breaker, but the decapitation of his wife seemed to me charged with cultural significance enough to warrant open-mindedness as to the identity of the perpetrators or the henchmen involved. If the severance of her head had been concomitant to the disposing of the body, there had to be a reason…

Miss Ling was 5' 8", a tallish woman, by any standard. Is it possible that her head had been cut off so she could fit in a car's boot? This research would also come handy in profiling, later on…

By October, when the case began to fester in the media with yet another bandwagon of slurred lies about the late police officer, the head had yet to be found…

A murder scene tells a story… It is where criminal intents converge to fit into a larger chronological pattern. First, the obvious isolated location meant some sort of rugged transport had to have been used. To their credit, with today's modern technologies, the police provided enough evidence to time and circumstantiate the murder with precision. This execution would have been signed by several perpetrators in a location nearby the locus of the dead. The body would then have been wrapped and transported to the scene…

Her fingertips were burnt, her teeth were missing but one, which suggested a cunning attempt at making the crime look like a mob assassination. I believe the police pursued this lead for far too long, to their demise. They couldn't ignore it, but among the worst possible outcome was the incrimination of the commissioner as a detour whereas he had been a person of interest from day one, which means his hierarchy must have considered him as a scapegoat.

In the scramble for a culprit, the police investigation must have shot itself in the foot chasing gangs. After several months of unsuccessful leads, no suspect could be framed, except Sir Tony who had a figment of an alibi and couldn't be charged for lack of evidence. The possibility that this line of enquiry was an intentional wild goose chase didn't escape me. This could have been an internal matter up to the point where I would have been hired to help.

The body was discovered by two ramblers. It could have been Andrew and I. The Yorkshire Dales were our playground for a while before we got on to bigger and better climbs like Ben Nevis, in Scotland. Even now, as I write, I am convinced that what looked like a panicked drop and a false attempt at erasing DNA evidence was in fact a raspberry blown at Sir Tony…

Do I think like the Independent Police Complaint Commission, the IPCC, as it was called at the time, that Sir Tony had led the investigators astray? I certainly had the impression that he had led me down the path… If he was the murderer, he must have counted on his force considering him as a suspect only to be discounted later down the line with a credible alibi. It made sense. That is another option I could not disregard, knowing Sir Tony.

But I wanted to know more about his wife. Before I set off for the Moors and the crime scene for some well-needed psychic resonance work, I wanted to connect to her personal story. Of course, I meant to use ESP around the crime scene, but I surmised that Sir Tony's last will had to be honoured first, no matter what.

So, what did our Hong Kong debutante get herself into that warranted such punishment? The diaries told me so much that the administrative records couldn't!

I've just had a snoop at today's local press, and my friend, the evangelist pastor who helped me in the Kinder Scout cases won his appeal. We're all corrupt in the eyes of God. Make no bones about it. But, to find out that this man was a wolf in sheep's clothing and a fraudster was hard to believe… I also meant to call his wife as soon as the dust settled. It is probably best if I waited. Here I am, digressing again… Today and the past few weeks, at the church cafe, I couldn't remember if I paid for my coffee or not. As it happens, Tim's church runs a cafe on Market Street too and I have my mid-morning coffee there every day. That is where I occasionally met the evangelical pastor. It did occur to me he was posing as a grandee, always dapper, but to imagine he was living it large off the Chapter! I still can't imagine Tim as a self-anointed peddler or a succubus who lived off the generosity of his congregation for his self-aggrandisement. Then again, you can't judge a book by its cover. That is why I always recommend my flock not to make any hasty judgments about anyone, let alone themselves…

Now, the diaries are hearsay and not admissible as evidence. But Sir Tony kept it under his hat for a reason, and police reports were all very nice, but I still had a dead man's wish to honour. To prove Sir Tony's innocence, I needed other leads, so I finally decided to visit the crime scene and make a good rambling of it too. The Google itinerary to Skipton was simple enough, but the weather forecast promised drenches of rain. I would drive the whole way to Skipton via George's pub and add the mileage from Sir Tony's mansion from there.

Skipton was the perfect place to start. That is where I aimed to basecamp before heading to Grassington and the crime scene nearby. Andrew couldn't make it at such a short notice. As I always rolled with the punches, I decided to go it alone. Spending some time in the quarry would enable me to impregnate the crime scene with some well-needed prayer.

Love Is a Diamond

Is love innumerable? How many facets are there to what humans call love?

"Philia", brotherly love, "storge", familial love, "eros", sexual attraction and "agape", divine love… It's all Greek to me… I know only one love: the love of humanity, which is indivisible as my love for my dearest, of course. No finger pointing ever.

Sir Tony is back on track now, as much as physically possible, of course.

This afternoon, I have had to go back to his diary, in between the snippets of borrowed times the News always manages to rob you of, and I remember that I decided to jump to the very last days before the murder, which I was led to believe was a crime of passion, before heading for the Yorkshire Moors…

Not only was I to rally to this interpretation of Helena's murder and tragic tale of death, but I was to exonerate Sir Tony due to lack of evidence.

But the justice I serve is not of this world… It is in this frame of mind that I resumed my scouring of the lovers' diaries, just one last time…

Sir Tony's writing was erratic, slipshod, and altogether confused before the night of the 20th of September. It is even violent at times. He recalls an argument with his wife prior to her death where they are both standing in the lounge, curtains drawn at 3 pm, as if night had fallen on their interior in the middle of the day.

It had been raining heavily for the past few days and Sir Tony's hunting trip had been cancelled. He had strong words with his wife about her planned city break the following weekend and wanted to confront her about it. The prospect of another sexual romp with her lover made him furious at first, but she sweet-talked him into accepting her infidelity as a mid-life crisis.

It wasn't the first time Sir Tony had turned a blind eye, but this time, she wanted a whole weekend off, only a week before their anniversary. They made love automatically, she recalls herself in her diary, like two servile automats responding to the call of a disjointed cuckoo, for appearance's sake, it seems…

By then, I was comparing the two diaries side by side…

Her English, tainted with Chinese idioms, tells how cleverly she had turned a confrontation into a moratorium, then a consensus. But she had doubts too… Her lover was coming into town, and as much as she had taken to the challenge with headstrong confidence, she feared her defiance might do more than just spice things up this time around…

Yet, it had to go ahead, as she saw it as part of a bigger plan to live her love life fully.

'How did it come to that?' she asks in the ultimate last pages. Could there be a way-out for her and her lover? The night before her disappearance, she booked a room at

George's pub. George being Sir Tony's cousin, she tells of her excitement at the daring move. George wouldn't find out about the lovers' daring escapade until the night in question, but all the more exciting for her, she writes.

As he followed Helena to George's gastropub, Sir Tony found out that very night that she was planning to leave him for good. Over the two days surrounding the disappearance of his wife, Sir Tony made no entry in his diary. He was busy no doubt… I didn't have the time to ask Sir Tony's schedule during those days before the fatal night, but Andrew told me that there had been a series of stabbing in Manchester, and Mike Crompton was breathing down his neck yet again. By Sir Tony's orders, the government had dispatched most of Greater Manchester police force under the Met's remit…

Sir Tony had worked all Saturday, visiting the area where anti-Muslim protests had flared up amidst heavy media presence. The last entry into Helena's diary is a Friday. She recounts her shopping trip to Old Trafford where she thought she saw someone who looked like Victoria Beckham. I checked; the Beckhams were in California at that time. You may wonder why I checked such an insignificant fact. I wonder too… I have become a webworm recently. Anything goes, from how a prostate works to satellite maps of countries I will never visit. It keeps me vigilant.

How a woman's mind could lead to her death is more interesting as I firmly believe Helena might have staged her own end. I remained non-judgmental at this stage of the enquiry. But it seemed to me that Helena knew what she was doing…

Before my trip to Skipton the next day, I had to visit the gay district. I had read news that the last secular bastion of intolerance towards gay people had come down in Scotland… Adrian's wall had been breached. I had to keep an open mind…

According to Andrew, Helena's lover was obviously queer, if a reclaimed one, and an affluent estate agent trading in Manchester, who visited his local on Friday nights, a New York style loft bar named after a neighbourhood in Manhattan, in the Gay village, on Canal Street.

Although, I had never met Rupert before, the idea of looking for a stranger among the dimly lit sofa beds of a trendy gay bar excited me. I remember being groped by a stranger in a nightclub once, and how we laughed it off with my friends who jumped at the opportunity to deride the quid pro quo at my expense.

This time around, I could dress in full collar shirt and cassock to better blend among the fancy dressed customers. I suppose if I didn't wear the gown and cap, I could pass for a cheerful reveller. But I came back to my senses in front of the mirror and decided for a standard black shirt instead.

Friday night came along and Andrew confirmed that he would be accompanied by his wife, despite his reservations. Not so much in terms of the village itself but the intelligence that was circulating about yet another terrorist attack against the LGBT community. As for I, I had not been out of my head for a while, and I was looking forward to go out.

On the night, Andrew, his wife and I met in Piccadilly station… We had some mulled wine on the way, strolling through Piccadilly gardens, and the Christmas market, before heading out to the Gay village. Seeing his wife filled me with joy. Her and I had a special connection. She had come back from a hen do in Morocco and was radiant.

Before long, Andrew spotted Rupert in the busy pub, and I initiated an impromptu conversation about the extraordinary décor of the bar. I needed to meet the guy. Of course, I had knowledge of his whereabouts the night of the murder, namely that he stayed at the hotel, as planned, with Helena alias Miss Ling.

I had to cross eyes with the fellow who saw her last. Before I told Rupert of my being a vicar – he seemed keen on chatting me up despite my age – I played along to his sexual banter and asked him about his previous relationships. We commingled with the crowd queuing at the bar before sitting down on the promiscuous couches laid for the indolent clientele. The conversation edged on Helena, but before I had a chance to ask him about the brass tacks of the case, Andrew made me a sign. His wife wanted to move along; the gay night had worn her out. I took his phone number, under the pretence that I was interested in his advances.

A bomb exploded at a pub nearby killing 15 people while we were walking back to the car park. A terrorist attack was what Andrew feared the most. He stayed behind while I accompanied his wife, Jane, back to a taxi station.

I returned to the Gay village once Jane was safe, but I could see by the look on her face that I had become a bird of ill omen in her eyes, due to my reckless investigation. I left Andrew to his work after helping a couple make it to the ambulances, and in the early hours, took a train back and reflected on my attitude towards the secular world in a black cab that charged me a fortune. I had to broaden my spectrum on the case before it wore me out too.

◆◆◆

The next day, as I was packing the car for my journey to the moors, I had a thought for the poor revellers at the Gay village, as some of them had been killed while dancing.

After a long prayer in my lobby, I had a strong urge to buy a coffee for the road to Skipton and Helena's crime scene. I couldn't dwell in mourning. I had to admit that time was of the essence. Andrew had quite a lot on his plate too. I decided to make a detour by the church cafe. When I arrived, Tim was there. We exchanged pleasantries and sat down. He mentioned the possibility of doing some community service on account of his good standing and the petty amount involved. We talked about the terrorist attack and how it felt like the noose was getting tighter around our Christians neck. We talked at length about honesty.

Tim was going to be okay, after all. I was relieved... These past few days, I told Tim, I officially began speaking to myself. My deep intimate self seemed ready to erupt, bubbling under the surface. I had been waiting for that moment when my hair would turn grey. Those signs are not signs of aging. They are the recognition that you are ultimately alone in the world, and that someday, you will leave this world as you came, wrapped in cloth. Aging is a natural conditioning process. It is not the fear of growing old. It is the fear of death, of infinite space. At 60, you can tell yourself the truth. You can take it. Lies don't cut it anymore. At 60, there is no time to waste; no clouds overcast the blue sky of your thoughts with fancy rainbows. To speak to oneself is an achievement in reconciliation. I told Tim that I had begun pestering against gravity too, and how objects tended to fall, and how the physical world always managed to wind you up and rub your nose in it.

There are multiple ways where negative energy can circulate in the physical world, he explained. If this negative energy is not recycled into a stream of positivity, crimes happen. My job as a vicar is to do just that, I told Tim who was as cheerful as ever. I am the bin man working for God's Green Council services. I wasn't using Sir Tony's case as a back pay for my personal experience, but a little trope never hurt anyone.

On the M60, I drew from my personal love life to try and come to terms with the crime of passion theory before I could turn to the macabre method of disposing of the body and its significance.

A while ago, Koroshiya was away for a conference or a seminar. She was staying at a hotel for a few days, over a weekend. It was in August. The conference came out of the blue. I could distinctly remember the email now.

Over the summer, she had been staying at her mum's more often. We rarely called each other and only communicated by emails when she was away. We never talked over the phone because we had agreed not to disturb each other due to our heavy work schedule. I hated being disturbed by a phone call while working at my desk, and so did she. Koroshiya usually hanged up the phone when she was at work. We had come to the tacit understanding that there shouldn't be any phone calls between us during working hours…

As soon as I read the email, I sensed that something was out of sorts. Or, at least, I let it convince me that I should be worried. My brains began to extrapolate…

An exception to the no-phone call rule was when she forgot her key and called me to see if I was in. I did answer the phone in case it was an urgent church matter that couldn't wait, but my answer was brutal and coarse when I heard her voice. She promised that she would never call again under any circumstances from that day on. She was angry even if she recognised she was in breach of our agreement.

I remember reading that email and contemplating the depth of the communication void that had crept in between us, shaped by years of conjugal fatigue, and especially the phrase "I will be out of town for a few days, for a conference". It was a weekend.

I realised I was probably clutching at straws when three possible interpretations of her email began worming their way into my entitled male consciousness:

1) She was attending a conference.
2) She was attending a conference with a lover she met at work.
3) She was not attending a conference.

These were the basics logical interpretations any husband would have come up with after reading his estranged wife's email. Had there been a crime, any detective reading that email would have come to the conclusion that it was a motive for murder.

Had I been a murderer, I imagine that this email could have been a clue in a crime investigation. It would not be unreasonable to assume more results could be produced out of this jealous equation; the possibility that her email was announcing a short-notice conference and nothing more being the most straightforward one, was the less interesting.

However, in a cop's mind, given the nature of the relationship between the two lovers (Koroshiya and I), this conclusion might be unsatisfactory. So it follows that one can foresee a fourth possibility, and then a fifth; the fourth possibility in the present case being that she was at a conference, but meant to give me a warning that she intended to do as she pleased, which the short notice corroborated. I could only deduce that Koroshiya was being defiant.

The fifth explanation would have been that she intended to tell me indirectly that she was unfaithful…

Our example was unique, but was it? In my reasoning, the fifth possibility seemed a viable option. What if Helena spent the weekend with her lover and deliberately chose the bold excuse of meeting at Sir Tony's cousin to drop a few red herrings?

In that case, she could easily be taxed with sheer shameless effrontery, but no cop would come up with that solution, unless there was hard evidence that she taunted him.

Koroshiya and I shared everything, but in the case of Sir Tony, a derided imagination and cunning plotting could have led him into a trap. Needless to say, the psychic in me came to the fifth case straight away. In a crime detection setting, you need to envisage all the options to come to a motive, but rarely does one come to the motive of faking a murder.

In their jargon, this is called circumstantial evidence. However, even a mere *laissez-faire* agreement between a husband and a wife, however morally questionable from an outsider's point of view, is proof enough that a common understanding is in place, that they want their union to carry on officially.

Sir Tony and his wife had had an argument the week before Helena disappeared… This cannot be discounted, but without reading the diary of Helena, no one would have known about it. Unfortunately, there was no emotional probing or soul-searching on Sir Tony's part, neither in his diary, nor from the testimonies I managed to gather when I visited their neighbourhood. I must assume that he was played.

When she was first advised by her husband to write a diary and improve her English, Helena wrote about her loneliness in a foreign country, her husband taste for rough sex and extra-marital pleasures, comforted only by a pragmatic hope that, with patient abnegation, their withering love could be reborn one day. Little did she know this would lead to his suicide after her death…

Yet, had he wanted to kill her, he would have made sure that these diaries were kept under wraps. His suicide didn't change anything to the equation, however deplorable…

What if he had called on my services with the intention to commit suicide? I didn't expect exclamation points and pencilled hearts or lightning bolts from Sir Tony's diary, but I wished he had been a bit more articulate about his emotions in his journalled demise. He should have bought himself a guest book instead.

Except for the argument with his wife, nothing seemed to be worthy of note about the last days of Helena's life. And finally, there was another possibility: what if she had sought to make him jealous to rekindle their Hong Kong flame or worse push him over the edge intentionally? This would explain why he followed her that night in view of all, risking a precious alibi. On the other hand, he may have intended to draw attention to himself that night, so an accomplice could do the dirty work for him. I had to visit the crime scene. Only my psychic gifts could bring light to this case.

The Bookshop

No sooner did I return from Skipton and the Moors that I received a call from Andrew.

'Hi, Andrew… What can I do you for you, maty?'

'How was your trip?'

'I've just come back… You're not following me, are you?' I had barely unpacked.

'No, I had you followed.'

'Ah. Ah. Ah… How is Jane since…?'

'Ah, she's okay. Thanks God she was bored! So how were the Moors, hey, nippy, was it?'

'Nippy? No, not at all… The weather was great. Listen, we need to talk. I have made some progress. I talked to some locals. Most of them were either drunk or in a rush, but all the same, the crime scene visit has been fruitful, I am proud to say.'

'All, right, when do you want to meet then?'

Andrew and I decided to meet at the Dog and Partridge, for a change… There aren't decent pubs in New Mills. Robinson's, the brewers, killed them all, except for that spineless moustached hypocrite who owns the Royal Oak. I make no apologies for it. I hate the scruffy racist son of a bitch. God have mercy…

On my way to the Dog and Partridge, I heard a loud cackle in the sky and watched a flight of geese. It warmed my heart to know things never change. I love my little town. It is vibrant, yet peaceful, and somehow, I know I owe that to Robinson's…

Helena bled to death of course. Her blood seeped into the wet autumn grass cushion. I was standing in the field, on the spot where her body had been deposited like a doom's day harbinger.

The place left an imprint on my soul… The little I learned from my visit of Grassington, near Skipton, at the verge of the Yorkshire dales, I realised it had stared Andrew and his team in the face. On the very morning I went to visit the scene by foot, I walked past a bookshop where I was arrested in my tracks, as if magnetically drawn in by a window display. Right there, just a couple of 100 yards from the B&B, I found Lord Irving's picture on a book cover that caught my attention. It was him, no doubt about that. But his nom de plune was Herbert Sullivan.

Why the shop window caught my attention, I do not know. But the overwhelming sense of purpose I felt on the crime scene had now formed into concrete conviction. I first thought it must have been Lord Irving's doppelganger, as there is always one. But the arcane procedures of my intuition weren't in question here since the name and the book were right in front of me.

Since it was too early to find out more about the usurper who nagged me behind the window from its unworthy pedestal, I had a cup of coffee at Costa's and waited until the bookshop opened…

The rest is what Andrew rightfully described as a ludicrous scam. Lord Irving had written a book about the murder of his wife, and no one knew about it. Andrew burst out laughing when I told him that I had been planning to go to Hong Kong to look into Miss Ling's past…

But it's the locals at a pub I visited on my first night who gave water to my mill…

Lord Irving had been in the area, according to one solicitor whom I met during my evening meal after my crime scene meditation. She was sitting next to me, working on a case in front of a glass of wine. We talked at length about the discovery of the crime scene as soon as I told her I knew Sir Irving. How we came to discuss it is all down to my frankness and forthright nosiness. I looked over her shoulder to see what she was working on and noticed she was a solicitor. I am long-sighted and can read small Arial script at three feet.

She had graduated in criminal law and the case news still tainted the peaceful landscape of Skipton with a bone-chilling dye.

'How could you have missed that?' I teased Andrew, in front of two foamy stouts.

'We didn't look in the right places, it seems,' he answered, his double chin wobbling with obfuscated resignation.

'So, motive, opportunity, it's all there, even, means.' I insisted, getting back at Sir Tony's doppelganger.

'Yeah, but we couldn't place him there on the night of the murder now could we?' he said, vindictively.

'Not if you don't look carefully, you sod. Are you sure of the time of death?' I asked incredulously.

‘Well, now you mention it. She could have been killed by someone else for him to finish the job with an axe later. But the autopsy report doesn’t indicate anything of the sort. Just…’ Andrew stopped in his tracks, as a rabbit caught in the headlights.

‘What Andrew? Just what do you mean by “just”?’ I said looking him square in the eye, as he now probed the gaping hole of his brain.

‘Just that… The head was chopped off a few hours after the time of death and that it wasn’t the cause of death.’

‘That’s that then,’ I said, ironically.

‘Yep,’ said Andrew, knocking his beer back thoughtfully before picking a brown pitted olive from a bowl.

‘But how was it chopped off, exactly?’

‘A hatchet or a cleaver… I need to work again on access. It’s all very well to have the motive and opportunity, but there’s still access,’ he said munching away…

‘Right, and did you find the autopsy report on Helena’s body?’

‘That’s the thing I wanted to tell you about,’ he said, suddenly grave.

‘It seems it’s been conveniently misled.’

‘You’re 100% sure of that?’

‘I mean access is still a problem.’

‘Yes, but unless I solve that head conundrum, I can’t start a crusade.’

‘Sure. I’ll see what I can do…’

I also asked Andrew to revisit the methodology of access to the crime scene. It meant a four-wheel drive or a similar motorised 2L plus engine had to have been used… There was no way anyone would have accessed the scene of discovery without a relatively powerful engine. But Andrew would cover that side of the case files…

I felt as if I had been having a tête-à-tête with the head of the paperclips and staples department in some big stationery chain, looking at endless rows of printing paper and plastic folders. Poor Andrew…

Could Irving have killed his wife to promote his book? Nah…

As I found out reading the book, which told the story of his love affair with the late transvestite, Lord Irving was blaming the government and some royal conspiracy hunt against the Hong Kong socialite who knew too much about some British prince's tax evasion scheme. A scandal is all Sir Irving wanted for his career as an author to thrive…

Andrew and I parted well after 10 pm. He promised to look at the autopsy report once more. I could still see his hollow emaciated eyes screwed into his sagging shoulders, his neck crowned with a black turtleneck that accentuated his pale complexion and droopy jaws in the glass partition of the pub's booth. Andrew was on a diet…

All cops will tell you that a medium's visions are always only relevant retrospectively. You could call it a space-time catch 22. If there's one thing I have learned in my career as a psychic is that you can't rush the dead, but my vision on the crime scene had materialised in this discovery of the book Sir Tony had written to describe the murder and I wouldn't be blamed for doing my job well…

Indeed, if there was one thing I had learned from this expedition, it was that Helena alias Miss Ling had more fingers in pies that the original autopsy report dared to state.

However, it now became clear that Sir Tony had sent me his diaries as part of an afterlife PR stunt. Whom did he want to hurt after his death? Deciphering his morbid joke was no skin off my nose, provided I would solve the case, but using a chip off the old Bible block to pursue your own ends was a different kettle of fish altogether!

The Resurrection

I love hearing preachers talk about Jesus and the resurrection. Just thinking about it makes me salivate. All claim without exception before their law-abiding congregation that "Jesus died for our sins".

This fallacious deal cannot be further away from the truth… By saying 'Jesus died for our sins', you give to whosoever wishes so a pretext to waste their fruitful life, a blank cheque for all manners of licentious behaviour.

It is a seducing and vindicating statement, no doubt. But joke aside (by that I mean Sir Tony's deathbed confession), what they seek is to bestow upon their flock a false sense of empowerment so as to better shape them into the sinners they might not have been before stepping into a church for the first time.

It's a point in case, the absentee's burden of proof in the most read case files in the world. It is the oldest trick of the trade: the carrot and the stick…

'Oh sorry, I am a sinner, but thanks to Jesus, I am not anymore, well thanks a million… What is that going around the pews, a bucket? Oh, I see…'

But no matter what you do, when you walk out of church, you'll never be the same again.

Resurrection is a political trope meaning renewal. It is the renewal of the covenant between God and his people. Jesus died for the sins of Satan, not man. Believing literally leads you nowhere. He died on the cross to prove Satan was a free-falling seed of dissent and that it was time to upset the apple cart on the marketplace.

It is the true message of the Bible. There's no place for irony or complacency in the saviour's testament. The Bible is not a blank cheque. What you see is what you get. And what you don't get is a blank cheque.

Now that I had all the pieces of the puzzle laid out in front of me, as usual with puzzles, my first reaction was to be dumbfounded. I could only come to the conclusion that Sir Tony never meant for his wife's murder to be solved. It was a farce…

Besides, even without the autopsy report, which I could expect to be misleading, Helena had faked her death. If Sir Tony's book had been written before his wife's murder, I couldn't dispense reading it, nor taking it at face value. In fact, even the press would later get wind of the book and resurrect the case… If anything, Sir Tony could only be blamed for commandeering a clever drum-beating marketing campaign around the murder of his wife. He had even bought a Google campaign, I later discovered…

It now dawned on me that they could have planned the whole business together.

It was the second time the hairy descendant of a long lineage of divine right charlatans ruined my heavenly cruise. I had no reason to disbelieve my intuition now. The problem was proving it for the likes of Andrew.

◆◆◆

Winter snows came later due to a spell of hurricanes and global-warming related phenomena. A bush of roses I had planted following the Kinder Scout cases was still in bloom at the beginning of October. I should have known better… By the New Year, I had read the diaries, the book and all the case files. But I was no closer to a rational breakthrough. That is what aggravated me the most.

In fact, Andrew added fuel to the fire by spreading rumours about my police work in church. Not only had he been indiscrete, although not intentionally, but he had also violated police regulations. This one dilemma too many pushed me over the edge and my sermons echoed my impatience…

"Power slut" was published 10 days before Helena died. It is the story of a woman whose unbounded lust for power leads her to her death. Power, argues Herbert Sullivan (Sir Tony's unassuming pseudonym) has replaced "eros" among women who will stop at nothing to eradicate the male genus. He explains how even their sexual pleasure is faked as they only seek to become self-sufficient and self-serving succubus. The world, he admits, is prey to a self-destructive pattern justified in part by overpopulation and the dilemma of procreating. But this is not the reason why women find comfort in sex toys or female alter egos to satisfy their desire, he argues in his sociological fiction: the female sex is out to rule the world on its own.

I recognised in his "end of days" pattern some fragments of his wife's diary. Sir Tony's dabbling with fictional writing was in no way extraordinary or groundbreaking, but the character playing her husband plots a murder only to be beaten to the post by unknown assassins from an activist group called "Eve's angels".

Andrew and I met again at the Dog and Partridge, a week later, to regroup around the case. Andrew was reluctant to be cross-examined once more on the face of his police work... The air was dense with mist, the trees strangely still after the tail end of the hurricane, but the Dog and Partridge seemed like a beacon in time, a landmark no one could deny or circumvent, or avoid mentally.

As a vicar, I always realised that the real church in a town or a village is the local pub. Whoever the government might be, they would always find abiding citizens full of respect for their leaders in a church, but the shadow democracy devoted to the real stuff of life sits in a pub.

'But where do you find all this information?' asked Andrew, as we sat in a hangover corner of the Dog and Partridge.

'Didn't I tell you about ESP?' I said, bemused by the post-Brexit Machiavellian sentiment pervading the atmosphere in the pub and the press.

If Sir Tony's book wasn't the admission of guilt we were all looking for, there was a line in it that struck me: "A sow, after washing, always return to wallowing in the mire." Peter's proverb from the New Testament might have described Sir Tony's feelings about his wife, but, apart from a scintilla of a jealousy motive, nothing seemed to suggest that he had effectively carried it through. Not one event in the fictional tale written by Herbert Sullivan matched the case. We were back to square one at the Dog and Partridge with a possible cover-up and a head still rolling in the moss...

‘Where’s the head?’ I asked Andrew, out of the blue.

‘What, you want a refill?’ he suggested humorously.

‘You know what I mean.’

‘It was found in a skip near Bolton, it’s in the case files…’

‘Is it?’

‘I’m joking, it’s not, that’s right, because it was found recently, you’re right. I’ll email it to you.’

The Times paper that lay on the table attracted my attention away from Andrew’s glaucous humour and flimsy blond thatch. I knew the drill with my friend Andrew: munching olives was a self-hypnotic and comforting habit he took exception not to hasten…

While the gloomy trencherman stuffed himself with snacks, I opened the paper to find the article attached to the picture that had caught my eye. “A paradise at a stone’s throw” was the title of this article about a paper trail of tax avoidance among the entitled nobility of Britain. The glossy picture evoking a palm-tree paradise made me dream.

It had to be a sign from God…

‘What if the body found wasn’t Helena’s?’

‘What are you saying?’

‘Don’t choke Andrew, I’m serious, what if Helena was still alive? This would explain the head went missing until now, whose is it really?’

‘From what I can recollect, despite just having a quick look, the odontology confirms her identity.’

‘I mean how sure can you be with forensic odontology?’

‘Actually, only one tooth remained. I thought of asking Mike, but I have been pretty busy with the homeless boy murdered in Manchester recently.’

'Can you look into it? Check if the dentist is forensically qualified and all that?'

'Due diligence … Sure…'

Andrew would oblige with alacrity.

Despite my thorough medical terminology knowledge, I went straight to the medical examiner's opinion which is the layman's version of the report, as soon as it came through the post…

Saddened that the lovely long-legged post-woman had been replaced with the usual goody-two-shoes, I could not help noticing under the pathological findings, mention of the gastric mucosal petechial haemorrhages, or what they call Wischnewsky lesions, indicating cold storage or exposure to freezing cold…

Those dark brown or black spots found on the victim's liver meant the pathologist could interpret Helena had suffered hypothermia. I remembered that from the Kinder Scout cases, when they analysed the preserved bodies of so-called Victorian victims.

But how cold? The temperature in the moors could not have been lower than -5°C at the time of death. It wasn't enough to explain those dark menacing lesions. Yet, the police concluded that the cause of death had been environmental hypothermia.

After some research, I discovered that in some cases, those lesions could be attributed to diabetic ketoacidosis. In short, the same pathology could be found on the organs of diabetics who run short of insulin. As for the dental record, only one tooth remained, and after a counter-expertise paid by my church funds – I know I shouldn't have and it sounds ludicrous, but Andrew couldn't help me due to his flailing

status in the police department – a qualified forensic odontologist told me it was an implant once the pictures obtained by Andrew finally reached my office...
Not only did it look like a recent implant, but the tooth could never have been implanted post-mortem told me the forensic odontologist.

I may be getting long in the tooth, but Helena could still be alive if the tooth wasn't hers... It now made sense ... Why would the murderer(s) only leave one tooth?

I decided there and then not to let Andrew know about my theory until I had certainty. After all, he had been indiscrete. Actually, this was now my case, and no one else would rob me of my work this time. Not even Mike...

As I partayed with the blood of Christ, the next Sunday, it dawned on me that Andrew might have been told to bury the case, which might have explained the missing files. He could have been taken off the case for appearances' sake, to cover the hierarchy, when he came to my church with his tail between his legs.

Far from rejoicing in Andrew's demise, I could now see a pattern in the investigation that I had not anticipated. Sir Tony had identified the body. If the body found in the Yorkshire Moors wasn't the body of Helena, it had to be part of Sir Tony's master plan, and in that plan weighed the risk of self-incrimination and the need for a cover-up.

Paradise Lost

Paradise lost, haven found.

Repulse Bay, Hong Kong…

Once an eligible bachelor, Sir Tony visited the same bay, where old colonial eyesores were revamped and flanked with the essential English shopping Mall, during the golden 90's. Developed by the British, the bay was once a cutthroat where pirates plundered commercial boats on halt along the South China Sea coast… He had married here, in the same glossy paradisiacal Bay.

Mike Crompton had promised me a team to help in my investigation, but Helena's murder had been solved without his meddling, and I had kept the conclusions to my very entitled self…

The curse of the headless corpse was over. Sir Tony's shareholding in The Duke of Westminster's estate meant that he could have been in the same bathtub, trying to peer into the distance to find Macau as I was now… Except, he wasn't…

'You like the view?'

'I do…'

'Here is more champagne, sweetie.'

'Thanks.'

The idyllic bay made me nostalgic. I felt vindicated in usurping Sir Tony's private life, wallowing in his own bathtub, drinking his champagne…

Helena was not dead. On the contrary, she was well alive. It seemed to me that Sir Tony's lack of discretion and savoir-vivre, and by that, I mean, his incapacity to enjoy the good life, had been his demise. Helena was a she-male. He was married to a lovely creature, a marvel of nature which he somehow came to see as a monster or a freak as the spoilt prat he was.

I had read in his diary how his psyche suffered from her proximity, her contact and, how gradually, she had scrambled his self-image. He became confused about his own identity.

It was more a case of sexual quid pro quo. His confusion and dismay stemmed from the biological uncertainty of her sex. Little did he know Helena had met another hermaphrodite, a she-male like her with whom she had had a short fling…

The affair lasted a couple of weeks, but it was enough for Helena to contemplate her options with Sir Tony under a different light… So, she directed his suspicions to Rupert, whom one can assume was just a stooge. She made Sir Tony jealous at first, but her aim was always to embroil the estate developer into a property deal in Hong Kong. It was her backup plan. Her female genes bubbling under her skin, she also had a male appendage that could be useful to henpeck Sir Tony. As he became jealous and embarrassed, he became powerless…

Hence the publication of his book, another spoof to detract attention from the scandal in case she spilled the beans…

As soon as Sir Tony learnt of her affair with the estate agent, he upped the ante and became a partner in Rupert's property development business in Asia.

Simultaneously, Helena took advice from Rupert who even benefited from the pay-off, and before long, became a successful developer in Hong Kong too, only to find out Helena alias Ling was the sole beneficiary of Sir Tony's Asian fortune under probate laws in Hong Kong.

How odd and Machiavellian is it then, that Rupert, fifteen years younger than his distinguished cousin, should become Sir John's personal executor. How this yanked up twist came about is a mystery…

Indeed, Rupert had just been a steppingstone… She had never lost track of her ambitions to make it in British society and bring the bacon back to Hong-Kong, her place of birth.

Miss Ling had planned everything in minute and devilish details… She would just have to prove that she was alive against all odds to inherit his fortune…

I was never under any illusion about the nature of Evil, but as the great master says on the market place, on the day of Sabbath, a man is not defiled by what enters his mouth but what comes out.

In her diary, Miss Ling tells her of her hurt about Sir John's denigration of her true sex… 'Why', she asks, 'do we have to lie about who I am?'

Why indeed hide such a wonder of nature, gifted with the apparels of both sexes in such abundance…

◆◆◆

As I marvelled at the view from my pleasure vessel, ten floors above sea level, I couldn't help wondering who the wickedest of them all was…

The doom and gloom of limbo land was now far behind, and I pondered my chances of moving here permanently, at her side.

'It's a strange world,' I said, as she brought me a canapé.

'It sure is…' she said simply, composing her presence between our still and breathless words, as if some invisible orchestra was waiting for the next bar:

'We are just passing ships in this world…' she said.

'Just waiting in style,' I muttered.

'How else?'

'Don't worry, I am just enjoying myself… I am happy…'

'Good! Now, will you come out before your skin gets even more wrinkly?'

We laughed… It wasn't that odd that I should be replacing Sir Tony in her stead after all, but it was time to think about the few decades I had left to live, and this respite in my burdensome vicarious life would be pampered by her alter ego.

She had returned home to her native Hong Kong, and I had found her. I had always meant to come here, no matter how ridiculous Andrew thought the whole psychic escapade seemed to be from his standpoint…

I couldn't let Rupert get away with what he had done to that poor creature he became jealous of, and whom no one will ever know – Miss Ling wanted the name of her fling to be kept out of the mud – and needed some reflection time before getting back to my friend with the good news that I had cracked the case.

That bath felt like a watershed.

A moment later, I decided not to pursue this case further until I was sure in my heart that that was what I wanted. Sometimes, a finisher needs to leave things unfinished for others to enjoy the glory…

If I warned Mike Crompton about Rupert and Ling's alter ego, I could end up alone, embroiled in a toothless conspiracy rather than my bubbles of content. Then again, I didn't have to return until my skin became floppy and irreversibly crepey.

If Mike discovered Helena was alive, I would lose this gentile aura, this lulling sensation that one floats in sunshine, on a cushion of pure air, where the body is just a fleeting vessel, where out of love, it seems, time is suspended.

I decided I had no arbitrary decision to make. I would just let myself carried by the waves of this novelty feeling, a beautiful creature with a singing voice at my side, helping me drift leisurely into an ocean of vast incomprehension…